The Tragical History of Doctor Faustus

The Elizabe

By Christopher Marlowe

(1604)

Modernized in Spelling and Punctuation

With Supplemental Text

Annotated and Edited

by John D. Harris

Hungry Point Press
Wabasha • Minnesota

To my many memorable students:

Austin & Austin, Alex & Dawson (thanks for the cat), Anthony and Sydney, Jackson, Chloe, Adrien & Hailey, Dillon & well so many others whom this old man remembers fondly for their lovely faces but may have lost their names in the gradual disintegration we call the wisdom of age....

Introduction

The Tragical History of Doctor Faustus was Christopher Marlowe's last play. Newly written before his untimely and suspicious death in 1593, it was not yet complete and certainly not well-polished. Marlowe had tortuously labored the edits and creative amendments of his other poetic works (*Tamburlaine*, for example) for several years after first presentation. While many contemporary playwrights composed their dramas with sketchy outline and only select principle speeches were written to a script, actors left to *ad lib* much of the dialog – and this play shows just such a pattern – Marlowe characteristically published his own works with great care and sophisticated exaction and should have so finally published *Faustus* had he lived to complete it.

The surviving texts – the so-called A and B texts – are reconstituted from popular performances at some of the more prestigious London theatres, by impresario's there, to fix the canon of their fare, as much as to celebrate the play. Certain oddities to their differences can be supposed to be the invention of those who published them, and it is impossible to probate what is Marlowe's text apart from those passages which are identical. These identical passages – such as the closing speech of Faustus, or the speech "Was this the face that launched a thousand ships?" – may be inferred to be authentic Marlowe, much as the authentic words of Christ may be inferred from the identical passages in the various gospels, I suppose. And there is in both cases a stylistic integrity. But, as in both cases, we are left wishing we had an original autograph. The selection of one version over another is therefore just as much an aesthetic choice, as a technical one. Text A is not perhaps as reliable as Text B (according to some scholars) but I prefer its parts for reasons of some aesthetics—it is bawdier and more savory. In rendering it here, I have considered the differences to Text B and made such judicious modifications as seemed good, and as noted. But in the main, for whatever integrity it may be, what you find hereafter is Text A and I am not interested in exploring the scholarly disputes between the two for the sake of this play; they are not important.

Marlowe was undoubtedly inspired to write his play by folktales concerning the adventures of Johann Georg Faust, a real-life mountebank *cum* itinerant sorcerer who lived more-or-less contemporaneously to Martin Luther in Germany. Originally written down by an anonymous German author as a Protestant religious tract to serve as a moralistic cautionary tale upon irreligious and wicked self-aggrandizement, this artless book was published by Johann Spies in Frankfurt am Main in 1587 as *Faustbuch*. Its first English translation did not appear until the year after Marlowe's death, so it is possible that such passages in the play that may directly relate to this book are posthumous (therefore, specious). But the story of the play in the main is just as it was told in the German and was told in common folklore even before that German book appeared in any language, and thus Marlowe must have borrowed these, even if the English translation was not yet to appear.

Marlowe, always keenly intellectual in his literary approach, exploited the folktale in several important and controversial ways. First, the person of Johann Faustus is elevated to scholastic distinction, to be a reverend Doctor of Philosophy (indeed of Theology) of very great renown and one appointed to an eminent post in a famous University. Secondly, while the original protagonist would be "Faust" (which in German means "fist"), Marlowe deftly prefers "Faustus" so as to play upon its Latin meaning, "The Chosen One," as it were suggesting an ironical anti-Christ.

Other allusions to the legend of Simon Magus shall reinforce this thematic eponym. Magus had called himself "Faustus" (or *the chosen one* in Latin) according to Patristic legend and had been a pretender to the Holy See of Rome before Saint Peter who came to usurp him. Magus averred he could fly, and Saint Peter challenged him to prove it, whereupon his soaring flight into the blue sky, briefly astonishing his assembled Christians, was brought down by the stunning artillery of prayers from Saint Peter, hurled in a barrage against the devilish flying Magus who thence plunged to earth, crashed and died. In another fitting association with Magus according to his legend, this pagan-like would-be Christian bishop had taken to wife a certain whore in his hey-day, whom he claimed was the actual reincarnation of Helen of Troy; in just the same manner, Marlowe's Faustus would resurrect Helen by incantations to become his consort.

The allusion to Simon Magus was embedded in *Faustbook* whence Marlowe may have been inspired to exploit it. But Marlowe seemed to have relished the implications of a pagan effrontery, of atheistic arrogance, which the embrace of the legend may suggest. The subliminal tension of the drama is how Faustus edges this dangerous philosophy. Faustus's ambition for knowledge defies the limits of lawful speculation. It is not incidental, nor accidental, that Marlowe would shortly be arrested on charges of such similar heresies.

Contents

The Tragicall Histoy of the Life and Death

of Doctor Faustus.

With new Additions.

Written by *Ch. Mar.*

LONDON,
Printed for *Iohn Wright*, and are to be sold at his shop without
Newgate, at the signe of the Bible. 1620.

Frontispiece of early publication

The Tragical History

of Doctor Faustus

By Christopher Marlowe

(1604)

Text A (as edited)

The text is taken from the Quattro of 1604, reproduced on a web site by Tufts University. Spelling and punctuation have been modernized, and the text had been edited as noted. The so-called Perseus Digital Project contains a number of classic texts, made publicly available. The web address is www.perseus.tufts.edu.

The text of the drama in the A-Text version and B-Text versions are both available, individually and with cross-reference. The text of the *Faustbuch* is also available, individually and with cross-reference

Enter *Chorus*.

Not marching now in fields of *Thrasimene*,[a]

Where *Mars* did mate the *Carthaginians*,[b]

Nor sporting in the dalliance of love,

In courts of Kings where state is overturned,

Nor in the pomp of proud audacious deeds,

Intends our Muse to daunt his heavenly verse:[c]

Only this, gentlemen: we must perform

The form of *Faustus'* fortunes good or bad.

To patient Judgments we appeal our plaud,[d]

And speak for *Faustus* in his infancy.

Now is he borne, his parents base of stock,

In *Germany*, within a town called *Rhodes*:

Of riper years to *Wertenberg* he went,[e]

Whereas his kinsmen chiefly brought him up;

So soon he profits in divinity,

The fruitful plot of scholarism graced,

That shortly he was graced with doctor's name,

Excelling all, whose sweet delight disputes

In heavenly matters of theology,

---

[a] A battlefield in Italy where the Carthaginians defeated the Romans in 217 BC

[b] mate = side with

[c] daunt = control; rendered as "vaunt" in Text B

[d] "…appeal our plaud" = seek applause

[e] Wertenburg here refers to either Wittinberg or Württemburg, both of which were cities famous as hotbeds of the Protestant reformation in Germany.

3

'Til swollen with cunning, of a self conceit,[a]

His waxen wings did mount above his reach,[b]

And, melting, heavens conspired his overthrow;

For falling to a devilish exercise,

And glutted more with learning's golden gifts,

He surfeits upon cursed necromancy.

Nothing so sweet as magic is to him

Which he prefers before his chiefest bliss.

And this the man that in his study sits.[c]

    Exit.

    Enter *Faustus* in his Study.

Faustus Settle thy studies, *Faustus*, and begin

To sound the depth of that thou wilt profess;

Having commenced, be a divine in show,

Yet level at the end of every art,[d]

And live and die in *Aristotle's* works.

---

[a] cunning = knowledge. See also "self conceit": one of the first uses of the word "self" as a noun in the English language, rather than a pronoun. As a compound word, Marlowe consciously imitates a Greek usage. The late 16th century was the first occasion of the word "self-ish," employed as a term of moral vitriol by an English Puritan minister.

[b] A poetic allusion to the Greek myth of Daedalus who made wings of wax for his son to fly, but which melted as he approached the sun, so that he fell to his death.

[c] According to a 2016 Gallup poll of Americans, 61% say they believe in the existence of the Devil.

[d] level = aim

4

Sweet *Analytics* 'tis thou has ravished me:[a]

Bene disserere est finis logicis.[b]

Is to dispute well Logic's chiefest end?

Affords this Art no greater miracle?

Then read no more, thou has attained the end;

A greater subject fitteth *Faustus'* wit.

Bid *Oncaymaeon* farewell; *Galen* come:[c]

Seeing *Ubi desinit philosophus, ibi incipit medicus,*[d]

Be a physician *Faustus*, heap up gold,

And be eternis'd for some wondrous cure.

Summum bonum medicinae sanitas:

"The end of physic is our bodies health."[e]

Why, *Faustus*, has thou not attained that end?

Is not thy common talk sound aphorisms?

---

[a] *Analytics*, referring to Aristotle's Logic. Marlowe continuously alludes to Aristotle, suggesting Faustus' fascination with his ancient "natural philosophy." Aristotle's intellectual influence had grown steadily since the 12th century, along with commerce and war with the Arab nations that had preserved his writings; it renewed interest in the Greek language of the original New Testament. By the time of the Italian and English Renaissance (1450-1650), most of the important Greek texts had been rediscovered, and Greek became essential to a scholar's education, as much as Latin had always been. This remained largely true even into the early 20th century.

[b] "To argue well is the end of logic" (trans. from Latin; the original is Aristotle)

[c] *Oncaymaeon* is a glide of the Greek phrase, *on kai me on*, meaning "being and not-being"; it refers to a philosophical discussion by Aristotle. *Galen* is an ancient Greek who is famous for his treatises on medicine.

[d] "Where the philosopher leaves off, there the physician begins" (trans. from Latin)

[e] Faustus renders his own Latin translation; the original is from Aristotle.

Are not thy bills hung up as monuments,

Whereby whole cities have escaped the plague,

And thousand desperate maladies been eased?

Yet art thou still but *Faustus*, and a man.

Wouldst thou make man to live eternally?

Or, being dead, raise them to life again?

Then this profession were to be esteemed.

Physic farewell. Where is *Justinian?*[a]

Si una eademque res legatur duobus,

Alter rem alter valorem rei, &c.

A pretty case of paltry legacies:

Exhaereditari filium non potest pater nisi, &c.[b]

Such is the subject of the institute

And universal body of the Church.[c]

His study fits a mercenary drudge,

Who aims at nothing but external trash,

Too servile and illiberal for me.

When all is done, divinity is best;

Jerome's Bible, Faustus, view it well:[d]

---

[a] Justinian was a Christian-era Roman Emperor who promulgated a comprehensive and systematic book of laws; it became the basis for common law throughout Europe in the Medieval period.

[b] "If one and the same thing is bequeathed to two persons, one gets one thing and the other the value of the thing"; and then, "A father cannot disinherit the son except…" (trans. from Latin)

[c] Referring to Justinian's canon of law; the B Text uses the word "law" instead of "church."

[d] Saint Jerome translated the Greek New Testament into a serviceable Latin; it became the liturgical basis to the Roman Catholic Church while the Greek remained the sacred text for the

Stipendium peccati mors est. Ha! *Stipendium, &c.*[a]

The reward of sin is death: that's hard.

Si peccasse negamus, fallimur, & nulla est in nobis veritas.[b]

"If we say that we have no sin,

We deceive our selves, and there's no truth in us."

Why then belike we must sin,

And so consequently die.

Ay, we must die an everlasting death.

What doctrine call you this, *Che sera, sera*:

What will be, shall be? Divinity, adieu.

These Metaphysics of Magicians,

And Necromantic books are heavenly;

Lines, circles, scenes, letters and characters,

Ay, these are those that *Faustus* most desires.

O what a world of profit and delight,

Of power, of honor, of omnipotence

Is promised to the studious artisan?

---

church in Constantinople and in the province of that patristic influence.

[a] "The wages of sin is death." (trans. from Latin; Romans 6:23). Faustus omits the rest of the scripture, "…but the gift of God is eternal life through Jesus Christ our Lord." He is preoccupied, it appears, with physical annihilation.

[b] He translates in his following sentences. The reference is I John 1:8. Again, Faustus omits the apposition of the thought that immediately follows: "If we confess our sins, he is faithful and just to forgive us our sins…." Marlowe omits these for ironic effect, since virtually any Christian would know the reference and half-expect him to continue. Hence, Faustus defies the Word of God, posing a haughty argument by scripture against itself.

All things that move between the quiet poles[a]

Shall be at my command. Emperors and Kings,

Are but obeyed in their several provinces:

Nor can they raise the wind, or rend the clouds;

But his dominion that exceeds in this,[b]

Stretcheth as far as doth the mind of man.

A sound magician is a mighty god:

Here *Faustus* try thy brains to gain a deity.

      Enter *Wagner*.

Wagner, commend me to my dearest friends,

The German *Valdes*, and *Cornelius*;

Request them earnestly to visit me.

Wagner I will sir.

      Exit.

Faustus Their conference will be a greater help to me,

Than all my labours, plod I ne'er so fast.

---

[a] The *quiet poles* are those fixed and immovable anchors to the world, around which all turns. The cosmology of Faustus retains the medieval belief in an earth-centered universe. He does not believe the idea of a solar system, as expounded by Copernicus in 1543, and known to Marlowe. To the extent that Faustus is a heretic, it is not by his scientific views, despite his commitment to acquire true knowledge.

[b] exceeds = excels

Enter the *Good Angel* and the *Evil Angel*.[a]

Good Angel O *Faustus*, lay that damned book aside,

And gaze not on it, lest it tempt thy soul,

And heap Gods heavy wrath upon thy head,

Read, read the scriptures, that is blasphemy.

Evil Angel Go forward, *Faustus*, in that famous art,

Wherein all nature's treasury is contained:

Be thou on earth as *Jove* is in the sky,

Lord and commander of these elements.

Exeunt.

Faustus How am I glutted with conceit of this?[b]

Shall I make spirits fetch me what I please,

Resolve me of all ambiguities,

Perform what desperate enterprise I will?

I'll have them fly to *India* for gold,

Ransack the Ocean for orient pearl,

And search all corners of the new found world

For pleasant fruits and princely delicates;

I'll have them read me strange philosophy,

And tell the secrets of all foreign kings;

---

[a] One striking motif of an English morality play is the presence of these supernatural contestants. There will be other adaptations of such motifs and devices, as Marlowe deliberately incorporates that tradition.

[b] conceit = idea, or conception

9

I'll have them wall all *Germany* with brass,

And make swift *Rhine* circle fair *Wertenberg*;

I'll have them fill the public schools with silk,

Wherewith the students shall be bravely clad;

I'll levy soldiers with the coin they bring,

And chase the Prince of *Parma* from our land,

And reign sole king of all our provinces;

Yea, stranger engines for the brunt of war

Then was the fiery keel at *Antwerp's* bridge,

I'll make my servile spirits to invent.[a]

Come, German *Valdes* and *Cornelius*,

And make me blest with your sage conference.

Valdes, sweet *Valdes*, and *Cornelius*,

Enter *Valdes* and *Cornelius*.[b]

Know that your words have won me at the last,

To practice magic and concealed arts:

Yet not your words only, but mine own fantasy,

That will receive no object for my head,

But ruminates on necromantic skill.

Philosophy is odious and obscure,

Both law and physic are for petty wits;

---

[a] The Prince of Parma is a Spanish (and Roman Catholic) governor who had recently repressed rebellion (of Protestants) in the Netherlands; a ship ladened with explosives was exploded to destroy a bridge built by the Prince in Antwerp during its siege.

[b] *Cornelius* is Cornelius Agrippa, a famous medieval alchemist and magician (b. 1485 - d. 1535). *Valdes* is unknown.

Divinity is basest of the three,

Unpleasant, harsh, contemptible and vile,

'Tis magic, magic that hath ravished me.

Then, gentle friends, aide me in this attempt.

And I that have with concise syllogisms

Gravell'd the pastors of the German church,[a]

And made the flowering pride of *Wertenberg*

Swarm to my problems, as the infernal spirits,

On sweet *Musoeus* when he came to hell,[b]

Will be as cunning as *Agrippa* was,

Whose shadows made all *Europe* honor him.

Valdes *Faustus*, these books thy wit and our experience

Shall make all nations to canonize us:

As Indian Moores obey their Spanish Lords,[c]

So shall the subjects of every element[d]

Be always serviceable to us three,

Like lions shall they guard us when we please,

Like *Almaine* rutters with their horsemen's staves,[e]

Or Lapland giants trotting by our sides;

Sometimes like women, or unwedded maids,

---

[a] gravell'd = confounded, or "floored" them

[b] *Musaeus* was a mythic musician whose music would heal the
sick; hence, when he went to Hades, the dead thronged to him for
new life. See *Aeneid* (Book 6, line 667).

[c] Indian Moores = the native American Indian

[d] The natural elements are water, fire, earth and water. These are
represented and incarnate with corresponding spirits.

[e] Meaning, "German cavalry with lances"

Shadowing more beauty in their airy brows,

Than in their white breasts of the queen of love,

For *Venice* shall they drag huge Argosies,[a]

And from *America* the golden fleece,

That yearly stuffs old *Philip's* treasury,[b]

If learned *Faustus* will be resolute.

Faustus *Valdes* as resolute am I in this

As thou to live; therefore object it not.

Cornelius The miracles that magic will perform,

Will make thee vow to study nothing else,

He that is grounded in Astrology,

Enriched with tongues, well seen in minerals,[c]

Hath all the principles magic doth require.

Then doubt not, *Faustus*, but to be renowned,

And more frequented for this mystery,

Then heretofore the Delphian Oracle.[d]

The spirits tell me they can dry the sea,

And fetch the treasure of all foreign wracks,

---

[a] Argosies = a fleet of ships

[b] That is, King Philip II of Spain. The English were in and out of war with Spain at this time. Just a few years previous (1588), the English (and English weather) aborted an invasion of the England by a 130-ship Spanish Armada; it commenced a period of British sovereignty on the seas which lasted into the 20th century..

[c] well seen = well versed

[d] The Dephian Oracle was installed at the shrine of Apollo in Delphi in Greece. In the ancient world politicians, soldiers and ordinary persons visited it in great numbers for the instructions and soothsaying of the so-called Sibyl.

Ay, all the wealth that our forefathers hid

Within the massy entrails of the earth.

Then tell me, *Faustus*, what shall we three want?

Faustus Nothing, *Cornelius*; O this cheers my soul.

Come show me some demonstrations magical,

That I may conjure in some lusty grove,

And have these joys in full possession.

Valdes Then haste thee to some solitary grove,

And bear wise *Bacon's* and *Albanus'* works,[a]

The Hebrew Psalter, and New Testament,

And whatsoever else is requisite

We will inform thee ere our conference cease.

Cornelius *Valdes*, first let him know the words of art;

And then, all other ceremonies learned,

Faustus may try his cunning by himself.

Valdes First I'll instruct thee in the rudiments.

And then wilt thou be perfecter than I.

Faustus Then come and dine with me, and after meat,

---

[a] The Bacon in this reference is *Roger Bacon*, not Francis Bacon who is the Elizabethan scientist/essayist, but an earlier magician whose published book Marlowe must have known. *Albanus* here is probably the medieval scholar and alchemist, Albertus Magnus.

We'll canvas every quiddity thereof,[a]

For ere I sleep I'll try what I can do;

This night I'll conjure though I die therefore.

Exeunt.

.... **Scene 2** ....

Enter two *Scholars*.

Scholar I wonder what's become of *Faustus*, that was wont to make our schools ring with *sic probo*.[b]

Scholar That shall we know, for see here comes his boy.

Enter *Wagner*.

Scholar How now sirrah, where's thy master?

Wagner God in heaven knows.

Scholar Why, dost not thou know?

Wagner Yes, I know, but that follows not.

---

[a] canvas every quiddity = look into every particular; a "quiddity" from the Latin, *quid*, or "thing"

[b] "Thus I prove…" (trans. from Latin), a common expression for scholars making "disputations."

14

Scholar Go to,sirrah! leave your jesting, and tell us where he is.

Wagner That follows not necessary by force of argument, that you being licentiate should stand upon't, therefore [a]acknowledge your error, and be attentive.

Scholar Why, did'st thou not say thou knew'st?

Wagner Have you any witness on't?

Scholar Yes ,sirrah, I heard you.

Wagner Ask my fellow if I be a thief.

Scholar Well, you will not tell us?

Wagner Yes sir, I will tell you, yet if you were not dunces, you would never ask me such a question, for is not he *corpus naturale*, and is not that *mobile*, then wherefore should[b] you ask me such a question? But that I am by nature phlegmatic, slow to wrath, and prone to

---

[a] licentiate = a person holding a degree from a university, in this context. Wagner is mocking academic exchange of logic and wit.

[b] *Corpus naturale seu mobile* is the Aristotelian phrase to distinguish a thing of this world; it is natural and may be subject to motion or change, as opposed to the unchanging heavens or ideal forms.

lechery (to love, I would say), it were not for you to come within forty foot of the place of execution, although I do not doubt to see you both hang'd the next sessions. Thus having triumphed over you, I will set my countenance like a precisian, and begin to[a]

speak thus: truly my dear brethren, my master is within at dinner with *Valdes* and *Cornelius*, as this wine if it could speak, it would inform your worships, and so the Lord bless you, preserve you, and keep you my dear brethren, my dear brethren.

Exit.

Scholar Nay, then, I fear he has fallen into that damned art, for which they two are infamous through the world.

Scholar Were he a stranger, and not allied to me, yet should I grieve for him. But come let us go and inform the Rector, and see if he by his grave counsel can reclaim him.

Scholar O, but I fear me nothing can reclaim him.

Scholar Yet let us try what we can do.

---

[a] A *precisian* is a person who is "precise" in his religious observances, that is, he is a Puritan. Marlowe was anything but.

Exeunt.

.... **Scene 3**.........................

Enter *Faustus* to conjure.

Faustus Now that the gloomy shadow of the earth,

Longing to view *Orion's* drizzling look,^a

Leaps from th'antarctic world unto the sky,

And dims the welkin with her pitchy breath:^b

Faustus, begin thine incantations,

And try if devils will obey thy hest,

Seeing thou hast prayed and sacrificed to them.

Within this circle is *Jehovah's* name,

Forward and backward, anagrammatis'd,^c

The breviated names of holy Saints,

Figures of every adjunct to the heavens,

And characters of signs and erring stars,

By which the spirits are enforced to rise.^d

----

^a Again, the medieval cosmology where the sun moves around the earth, and so the earth casts its shadow to make the constellations visible. Orion, a winter constellation, was a huntsman in Greek mythology who was blinded and cursed for rape or other crimes.

^b "welkin" = vault of the sky or the very top of it; it originates from an Old English word for cloud.

^c A classic magic circle contains Yahweh's name in a criss-cross anagram.

^d *Erring stars* are "moving stars," that is, the planets. Faustus invokes the elements of the Zodiac. Astrology and the powers of its constituents were allied in mind with the other "spirits" of the air, such as demons and devils.

Then fear not *Faustus*, but be resolute,

And try the uttermost magic can perform.

Sint mihi Dei Acherontis propitii! Valeat numen triplex Jehovae! Ignei, aeriI, aquatani spiritus, salvete! Orientis princeps Beelzebub, inferni ardentis monarcha & Demigorgon, propitiamus vos, ut appareat & surgat Mephistophilis. Quid tu moraris? Per Jehovam, Gehennam, & consecratam aquam quam nunc spargo, signumque crusis quod nunc facio, & per vota nostra, ipse nunc surgat nobis dicatus Mephistophilis.[a]

Enter a Devil.

I charge thee to return and change thy shape;

Thou art too ugly to attend on me.

Go and return an old Franciscan Friar;

That holy shape becomes a devil best.

Exit Devil.

I see there's virtue in my heavenly words;

Who would not be proficient in this art?

How pliant is this Mephistophilis?

Full of obedience and humility,

---

[a] "Be propitious to me, gods of Acheron! May the triple deity of Jehovah prevail! Spirits of fire, air, water, hail! Beelzebub, Prince of the East, monarch of the burning hell, and Demogorgon, we propitiate ye, that Mephistophilis may appear and rise. Why dost thou delay? By Jehovah, Gehenna, and the holy water which now I sprinkle, and the sign of the cross which now I make, and by our prayer, may Mephistophilis now summoned by us arise!" (trans. from Latin) Gehenna is a Hebrew name for Hell. *Acheron* in Greek mythology is a river in Hell. This incantation is Marlowe's invention, or at least it is not present in any of the *Faustbuch* texts.

Such is the force of magic and my spells.

Now Faustus, thou art conjurer laureate

That canst command great Mephistophilis,

Quin regis Mephistophilis fratris imagine.[a]

Enter *Mephistophilis.*

Mephistophilis Now, Faustus, what would'st thou have
me do?

Faustus I charge thee wait upon me whilst I live,

To do what ever Faustus shall command,

Be it to make the Moon drop from her sphere,

Or the Ocean to overwhelm the world.

Mephistophilis I am a servant to great Lucifer,

And may not follow thee without his leave,

No more than he commands must we perform.

Faustus Did not he charge thee to appear to me?

Mephistophilis No, I came now hither of mine own
accord.

---

[a] "For indeed thou hast power in the image of thy brother
Mephistophilis." (trans. from Latin)

Faustus Did not my conjuring speeches raise thee? Speak.

Mephistophilis That was the cause, but yet per accident, For when we hear one rack the name of God,

Abjure the scriptures, and his Savior Christ,
We fly, in hope to get his glorious soul;
Nor will we come unless he use such means
Whereby he is in danger to be damned:
Therefore the shortest cut for conjuring
Is stoutly to abjure the Trinity,[a]
And pray devoutly to the Prince of Hell.

Faustus So *Faustus* hath already done, & holds this principle: There is no chief but only *Beelzebub*,[b]

To whom *Faustus* doth dedicate himself.
This word damnation terrifies not him,

---

[a] In 1593, a year or so after he had written this play, Marlowe is accused of heresy against the Trinity.

[b] The bestiary of Hell is a bit confusing. Sometimes the names are intermixed and refer to the same entity; sometimes they mean different demons. Historically, each name emerged of its own tradition. Beelzebub was a demon name derived from the deity named Ba'al, a god of Canaan which the Bible excoriates. Lucifer is a name which means "light bearer" and is associated with the morning star or Venus, for by legend it is an angel or spirit who sought to outshine all others. The legend of Lucifer or Satan as a rebellious angel is largely Christian lore that developed over many centuries after Europe had been converted.

For he confounds hell in Elysium;[a]

His ghost be with the old philosophers.

But, leaving these vain trifles of men's souls,

Tell me what is that *Lucifer* thy Lord?

Mephistophilis Arch-regent and commander of all
spirits.

Faustus Was not that *Lucifer* an Angel once?

Mephistophilis Yes, *Faustus*, and most dearly lov'd of
God.

Faustus How comes it then that he is Prince of devils?

Mephistophilis O, by aspiring pride and insolence,
For which God threw him from the face of heaven.

Faustus And what are you that live with *Lucifer*?

Mephistophilis Unhappy spirits that fell with *Lucifer*,
Conspired against our God with *Lucifer*,
And are for ever damned with *Lucifer*.

Faustus Where are you damned?

---

[a] *Elysium* is the ancient, largely Roman conception, for a happy
after-life.

Mephistophilis In hell.

Faustus How comes it then that thou art out of hell?

Mephistophilis Why this is hell, nor am I out of it.

Thinkst thou that I who saw the face of God,

And tasted the eternal joys of heaven,

Am not tormented with ten thousand hells,

In being deprived of everlasting bliss?[a]

O *Faustus*, leave these frivolous demands,

Which strike a terror to my fainting soul.

Faustus What, is great Mephistophilis so passionate

For being deprived of the joys of heaven?

Learn thou of Faustus manly fortitude,

And scorn those joys thou never shall possess.

Go bear those tidings to great Lucifer:

Seeing Faustus hath incurred eternal death,

By desperate thoughts against Jove's deity,

Say he surrenders up to him his soul,

So he will spare him four and twenty years,

Letting him live in all voluptuousness,

Having thee ever to attend on me,

To give me whatsoever I shall ask,

---

[a] This idea of Hell belongs to Thomas Aquinas. It is an intellectual conception, not at all the popular and naturalistic conception of a hell of eternal suffering and torment. Is Mephistophilis toying with Faustus? Or is this "passionate" demon truly regretful?

To tell me whatsoever I demand,

To slay mine enemies, and aide my friends,

And always be obedient to my will.

Go and return to mighty Lucifer,

And meet me in my study at midnight,

And then resolve me of thy master's mind.

Mephistophilis I will, Faustus.

    Exit.

Faustus Had I as many souls as there be stars,

I'd give them all for Mephistophilis.

By him I'll be great Emperor of the world,

And make a bridge through the moving air,

To pass the Ocean with a band of men;[a]

I'll join the hills that bind the African shore,[b]

And make that land continent to Spain,

And both contributory to my crown.

The Emperor shall not live but by my leave,

Nor any Potentate of Germany.

Now that I have obtained what I desire,

I'll live in speculation of this art,

'Til Mephistophilis return again.

---

[a] Again, a medieval conception of the cosmology; the land-mass of the world is singular and surrounded by the ocean; to bridge it is to rise from its western shore and set down on its eastern.

[b] That is, he will seal off the Mediterranean by connecting Europe and Africa.

Exit.

.... Scene 4 ....

Enter *Wagner* and the *Clown*.[a]

Wagner Sirrah, boy, come hither.

Clown How, boy? Swowns[b] boy! I hope you have seen many boys with such pickadevaunts as I have. Boy, quotha?[c]

Wagner Tell me, sirrah, hast thou any comings in?[d]

Clown Ay, and goings out too, you may see else.

Wagner Alas poor slave. See how poverty jesteth in his nakedness. The villain is bare, and out of service, and so

---

[a] The occasional scene wherein "clowns" appear served a number of purposes in Elizabethan drama. Derived from a device of morality plays that were featured at festive fairs, such scenes in that tradition meant to provide a comic break and keep the crowd watching. But, as this scene also suggests, they may serve a meaningful counterpoint to the drama, providing a common man's (or idiot's) view of the goings-on. A "clown" was term for a rustic or rural person, not a fool per se. Originally such scenes may have been ad-libbed by the players, although here whoever published this first version of *Doctor Faustus* has written it down.

[b] Swouns (zounds) = an elision for the exclamation "By God's Wounds"

[c] Pickadevaunts = a pointed beard, as the devil may have worn

[d] coming in = income or earnings

24

hungry that I know he would glue his soul to the Devil for a shoulder of mutton, though it were blood raw.

Clown How, my soul to the devil for a shoulder of mutton though 'twere blood raw? Not so, good friend. By'r Lady, I had need have it well roasted, and good sauce to it, if I pay so dear.

Wagner Well, wilt thou serve me, and I'll make thee go like *Qui mihi discipulus*?[a]

Clown How, in verse?

Wagner No, sirrah, in beaten silk and stavesacre.[b]

Clown How, how, Knaves acre? Ay, I thought that was all the land his father left him. Do ye hear? I would be sorry to rob you of your living.

Wagner Sirrah, I say in staves "ache"-er.[c]

Clown Oho! Oho! Stavesacre! Why, then, belike if I

---

[a] "You who are my pupil…" (trans. from Latin) is from a poem by W. Lily.

[b] Stavesacre = an herb used to repel lice

[c] Employing the pun, meaning to be beaten by a stick (or stave)

were your than I should be full of vermin.

Wagner So thou shalt, whether thou beest with me, or no. But sirrah, leave your jesting, and bind your self presently unto me for seven years, or I'll turn all the lice about thee into familiars, and they shall tear thee in pieces.[a]

Clown Do you hear sir? You may save that labour; they are too familiar with me already. Swowns! they are as bold with my flesh as if they had paid for my meat and drink.

Wagner Well, do you hear sirrah? Hold, take these guilders.

Clown Gridirons! what be they?

Wagner Why, French crowns.

Clown Mass, but for the name of French crowns, a man

---

[a] A *familiar* is a term for a personal spirit or devil. By folk lore one shall die from them by being torn apart alive. Faustus in the original *Faustbuch* meets his death in this manner.

were as good have as many English counters, and what[a] should I do with these?

Wagner Why, now, sirrah, thou art at an hour's warning, whensoever or wheresoever the devil shall fetch thee.

Clown No, no. Here, take your gridirons again.

Wagner Truly I'll none of them.

Clown Truly but you shall.

Wagner Bear witness I gave them him.

Clown Bear witness I give them you again.

Wagner Well, I will cause two devils presently to fetch thee away—*Baliol* and *Belcher.*[b]

Clown Let your *Baliol* and your *Belcher* come here, and I'll knock them, they were never so knocked since they were devils. Say I should kill one of them, what would

---

[a] A *counter* is a token in exchange for something of value, such as a beverage, but in itself it's worthless; as opposed to the *guilder* which was actually gold.

[b] Baliol, Belcher, etc. are more names for spirits.

folks say? Do ye see yonder tall fellow in the round slop, he has killed the devil, So I should be called Kill-devil all the parish over.[a]

> Enter two *Devils*, and the *Clown* runs up and
> down crying.

Wagner *Baliol* and *Belcher*, spirits away!

Clow. What, are they gone? A vengeance on them; they have vile long nails. There was a he-devil and a she-devil. I'll tell you how you shall know them: all he-devils has horns, and all she-devils has clefts and cloven feet.

Wagner Well, sirrah, follow me.

Clown But do you hear? If I should serve you, would you teach me to raise up *Banios* and *Belcheos*?

Wagner I will teach thee to turn thy self to anything, to a dog, or a cat, or a mouse, or a rat, or any thing.

Clown How! A Christian fellow to a dog or a cat, a mouse or a rat? No, no sir, if you turn me into any thing,

---

[a] Kill-devil = a reckless fool, like a dare-devil

let it be in the likeness of a little pretty frisking flea, that I may be here and there and every where. O, I'll tickle the prettie wenches plackets; I'll be amongst them, i'faith.[a]

Wagner Well, sirrah, come.

Clown But, do you hear, *Wagner?*

Wagner How! *Baliol* and *Belcher.*

Clown O Lord, I pray sir, let *Baliol* and *Belcher* go sleep.

Wagner Villain, call me Master *Wagner*, and let thy left eye be diamctrically fixed upon my right heel, with *quasi vestigias nostras insistere.* [b]

Exit.

Clown God forgive me, he speaks Dutch fustian. Well,[c] I'll follow him, I'll serve him, that's flat.

Exit.

---

[a] plackets = slits in petticoats, to permit a woman to urinate, etc.; probably here an obscene pun (cf. "clefts")

[b] "As if to tread in my tracks." (trans. from Latin)

[c] fustian = bombast or pretentious speech

Enter *Faustus* in his Study.

Faustus Now, *Faustus*, must thou needs be damned,

And canst thou not be saved?

What boots it then to think of God or heaven?

Away with such vain fancies and despair:

Despair in God, and trust in *Beelzebub*.

Now go not backward: no, *Faustus*, be resolute.

Why waverest thou? O, something soundeth in mine ears:[a]

Abjure this magic, turn to God again.

Ay, and *Faustus* will turn to God again.

To God? He loves thee not.

The God thou serv'st is thine own appetite,

Wherein is fixed the love of *Beelzebub*;

To him I'll build an altar and a church,

And offer luke warm blood of new borne babes.[b]

Enter *Good Angel* and *Evil Angel*.

Good Angel Sweet *Faustus*, leave that execrable art.

Faustus Contrition, prayer, repentance: what of them?

---

[a] His dialogue of conscience is perceived as a dialogue of spirits that buzzes in his ears.

[b] Ritual sacrifice of babies is an old allegation against heresy and occult practices, dating to the Patristic writers of the time of Constantine, the first Christian Roman Emperor.

Good Angel O, they are means to bring thee unto heaven.

Evil Angel Rather illusions, fruits of lunacy,
That makes men foolish that do trust them most.

Good Angel Sweet *Faustus*, think of heaven, and heavenly things.

Evil Angel No, *Faustus*, think of honor and wealth.

Exeunt. Angels

Faustus Of wealth,
Why the signiory of Emden shall be mine.[a]
When *Mephistophilis* shall stand by me,
What God can hurt thee *Faustus*? Thou art safe;
Cast no more doubts. Come, *Mephistophilis*,
And bring glad tidings from great *Lucifer*.
Is't not midnight? Come *Mephistophilis*,
Veni, veni, Mephastophile!

Enter *Mephistophilis*.

Now tell, what says *Lucifer* thy Lord?

---

[a] That is, the entitlement to taxable earnings from the city Emden, a wealthy port and site of commerce.

Mephistophilis That I shall wait on *Faustus* whilst he lives,[a] So he will buy my service with his soul.

Faustus Already *Faustus* hath hazarded that for thee.

Mephistophilis But *Faustus*, thou must bequeath it solemnly, And write a deed of gift with thine own blood, For that security craves great *Lucifer*. If thou deny it, I will back to fuel.[b]

Faustus Stay, *Mephistophilis*, and tell me what good will my soul do thy Lord?

Mephistophilis Enlarge his kingdom.

Faustus Is that the reason he tempts us thus?

Mephistophilis *Solamen miseris socios habuisse doloris.*[c]

---

[a] The A-Text reads "while I live…"; the B-Text reads "while he lives…" , which makes more sense.

[b] The idea of a contract or "deed of gift" with the Devil seems to be derived from an earlier legend, that of Theophilus of Cicilia (6th century) who made a pact with Satan in exchange for an ecclesiastical title. At his death bed, the Virgin Mother interceded in response to his prayers, snatching the document away from Satan, and begged God for his forgiveness. Theophilus was pardoned. This legend was well-enough known that it should be considered back-drop to the drama.

[c] Basically, "Misery loves company." (trans. from Latin)

Faustus Have you any pain that tortures others?

Mephistophilis As great as have the human souls of
men.But tell me *Faustus*, shall I have thy soul,

And I will be thy slave, and wait on thee,
And give thee more than thou hast wit to ask.

Faustus Ay, *Mephistophilis*, I give it thee.

Mephistophilis Then , *Faustus*, stab thine arm
courageously,And bind thy soul that at some certain day

Great *Lucifer* may claim it as his own,
And then be thou as great as *Lucifer*.

Faustus Lo, *Mephistophilis*, for love of thee,
I cut mine arm, and with my proper blood
Assure my soul to be great *Lucifer's*,
Chief Lord and regent of perpetual night,
View here the blood that trickles from mine arm,
And let it be propitious for my wish.

Meph. But, *Faustus*, thou must write it in manner of a
deed of gift.

Faustus Ay, so I will, but *Mephistophilis* my blood
congeals and I can write no more.

Mephistophilis I'll fetch thee fire to dissolve it straight.

    Exit.

Faustus What might the staying of my blood portend?
Is it unwilling I should write this bill?
Why streams it not, that I may write afresh:
Faustus gives to thee his soul. Ah, there it stayed,
Why shouldst thou not? Is not thy soul thine own?
Then write again: *Faustus* gives to thee his soul.

    Enter *Mephistophilis* with a chafer of coals.[a]

Mephistophilis Here's fire. Come, *Faustus*, set it on.

Faustus So now the blood begins to clear again;
Now will I make an end immediately.

Mephistophilis O, what will not I do to obtain his soul?

Faustus *Consummatum est*: this bill is ended,[b]
And *Faustus* hath bequeathed his soul to *Lucifer*.
But what is this inscription on mine arm?

---

[a] A *chafer* was a small stove or bucket with grate used to warm and for other purposes.

[b] "It is finished…" (trans. from Latin) from John 19:30; these are Christ's last words on the cross.

34

Homo fuge! Whither should I fly?[a]

If unto God, he'll throw me down to hell.

My senses are deceived; here's nothing writ:

I see it plain, here in this place is writ

Homo fuge! Yet shall not *Faustus* fly.

Mephistophilis I'll fetch him somewhat to delight his mind.

      Exit.

      Enter *Mephistophilis* with devils giving crowns and rich apparel to Faustus, and dance, and then depart.

Faustus Speak, *Mephistophilis*, what means this show?

Mephistophilis Nothing, *Faustus*, but to delight thy mind withal, And to show thee what magic can perform.

Faustus But may I raise up spirits when I please?

Mephistophilis Ay, *Faustus*, and do greater things then these.

---

[a] *Homo fuge* — "O man, flee…" — refers to I Timothy 6:11: "… O man of God, flee these things: and follow after righteousness, godliness, faith, love, patience, meekness."

Faustus Then there's enough for a thousand souls

Here, *Mephistophilis*, receive this scroll,

A deed of gift of body and of soul;

But yet conditionally, that thou perform

All articles prescribed between us both.

Mephistophilis Faustus, I swear by hell and *Lucifer*

To effect all promises between us made.

Faustus Then hear me read them: [a]

On these conditions following. First, that *Faustus* may be a spirit in form and substance. Secondly, that *Mephistophilis* shall be his servant, and at his command. Thirdly, that *Mephistophilis* shall do for him, and bring him whatsoever. Fourthly, that he shall be in his chamber or house invisible. Lastly, that he shall appear to the said *John Faustus* at all times, in what form or shape soever he please. *John Faustus* of Wertenberg, Doctor, by these presents, do give both body and soul to *Lucifer* prince of the East, and his minister *Mephistophilis*, and furthermore grant unto them that twenty-four years being expired, the articles above written in- violate, full

---

[a] The contract with the Devil in the *Faustbuch* is very similar. See the appendix in which it is reproduced. Specifically, the contract in the folk legend, like this one that Marlowe dramatizes, trades knowledge in exchange for his soul: "I haue not found through the gift that is giuen mee from aboue, any such learning and wisdome, that can bring mee to my desires: and for that I find, that men are vnable to instruct me any farther in the matter, now haue I Doctor *John Faustus*, vnto the hellish prince of Orient and his messenger *Mephostophiles*, giuen both bodie & soule, vpon such condition, that they shall learne me...." Marlowe, however, employs terms derived from Chapter 4 of *Faustbuch*, while the contract was under negotiation.

power to fetch or carry the said *John Faustus,* body and soul, flesh, blood, or goods, into their habitation wheresoever. By me *John Faustus.*[a]

Mephistophilis Speak, *Faustus,* do you deliver this as your deed?

Faustus Ay, take it, and the devil give thee good on't.

Mephistophilis Now, *Faustus,* ask what thou wilt.

Faustus First will I question with thee about hell;
Tell me, where is the place that men call hell?

Mephistophilis Under the heavens.

Faustus Ay, but whereabout?

Mephistophilis Within the bowels of these elements,
Where we are tortured and remain for ever,
Hell hath no limits, nor is circumscribed
In one self place; for where we are is hell,
And where hell is there must we ever be:

---

[a] Somehow it is fitting that a legalistic contract, the very emblem and signature of that emergent bourgeois capitalist age which now shall spur the Protestant reformation, is the centerpiece of the play. Contracts are of course essentially amoral, always representing the free will in free exchange—nothing, it is said, is wrong with what is freely agreed.

And to conclude, when all the world dissolves

And every creature shall be purified,

All places shall be hell that is not heaven.[a]

Faustus Come, I think hell's a fable.

Mephistophilis Ay, think so still, 'til experience change
thy mind.

Faustus Why? Think'st thou then that *Faustus* shall be
damned?

Mephistophilis Ay, of necessity, for here's the scroll
Wherein thou hast given thy soul to *Lucifer*.

Faustus Ay, and body too, but what of that?
Think'st thou that *Faustus* is so fond,
To imagine, that after this life there is any pain?
Tush; these are trifles and mere old wives tales.

Mephistophilis But, *Faustus*, I am an instance to prove
the contrary For I am damned, and am now in hell.

Faustus How! Now in hell? Nay and this be hell, I'll

---

[a] Cf. Lines 390 ff. Now another statement for the place of hell.
This scene parallels the *Faustbuch* in Chapter 20. However, in
Faustbuch, the description is vivid and more traditionally
expresses its horror.

willingly be damned here; what? walking, disputing, &c.? But leaving off this, let me have a wife, the fairest maid in *Germany*, for I am wanton and lascivious, and cannot live without a wife.[a]

Mephistophilis How, a wife? I prithee, *Faustus*, talk not of a wife.

Faustus Nay, sweet *Mephistophilis*, fetch me one, for I will have one.

Mcphistophilis Well, thou wilt have one. Sit there 'til I come; I'll fetch thee a wife in the devil's name.

Enter *Mephistophilis* with a devil
dressed like a woman, with fireworks.[b]

---

[a] See I Corinthians 7 where Paul relates that marriage is the only alternative to fornication. Otherwise, as Paul says, "… it is good for a man not to touch a woman." (I Corinthians 7:1) The episode wherein Mephistophilis discourages Faustus from marriage is found in Chapter 9 of the *Faustbuch*. His lechery is given great emphasis in the *Faustbuch*, while Marlowe makes his Faustus more constrained.

[b] The use of fireworks and the appearance of devils was good theatrics. The crowd paid for this. It is said that during one performance of *Doctor Faustus* in London, when the devils appeared, the audience panicked and ran from the theatre. Recall: this is a period in which plays had been occasionally banned because of the presence of deadly Plague that might be passed in contagion by these public gatherings. People were nervous, not to mention their genuine belief in devils.

39

Mephistophilis Tell, *Faustus*, how doot thou like thy wife?

Faustus A plague on her for a hot whore!

Mephistophilis Tut, *Faustus*, marriage is but a ceremonial toy; if thou lovest me, think no more of it.[a]

I'll cull thee out the fairest courtesans,
And bring them every morning to thy bed.
She whom thine eye shall like, thy heart shall have;
Be she as chaste as was *Penelope*,[b]
As wise as *Saba*, or as beautiful[c]
As was bright *Lucifer* before his fall.

Hold, take this book, peruse it thoroughly:
The iterating of these lines brings gold;
The framing of this circle on the ground
Brings whirlwinds, tempests, thunder and lightning.
Pronounce this thrice devoutly to thyself,
And men in armor shall appear to thee,
Ready to execute what thou desir'st.

Faustus Thanks, *Mephistophilis*, yet fain would I have

---

[a] "…think <u>no</u> more of it," as in the B-Text version; in the A-Text it reads "… think more of it"

[b] Penelope is the wife of the Greek hero, Odysseus, fabled for waiting twenty years for husband's return.

[c] The Queen of Sheba

40

a book wherein I might behold all spells and incantations, that I might raise up spirits when I please.

Mephistophilis Here they are in this book.

Turns to them

Faustus Now would I have a book where I might see all characters and planets of the heavens, that I might know their motions and dispositions.

Mephistophilis Here they are too.

Turns to them

Faustus Nay, let me have one book more, and then I have done, wherein I might see all plants, herbs and trees that grow upon the earth.

Mephistophilis Here they be.

Faustus O, thou art deceived.

Mephistophilis Tut, I warrant thee.

Turns to them.
Exeunt.

Enter *Robin* the Ostler with a book in his hand.[b]

Robin O, this is admirable! Here I ha' stolen one of doctor Faustus' conjuring books, and i' faith I mean to search some circles for my own use. Now will I make all the maidens in our parish dance at my pleasure stark naked before me, and so by that means I shall see more then ere I felt, or saw yet.

Enter *Ralph* calling *Robin*

Ralph *Robin,* prithee come away; there's a gentleman tarries to have his horse, and he would have his things rubbed and made clean. He keeps such a chafing with my mistress about it, and she has sent me to look thee out. Prithee come away.

---

[a] This scene is removed from the original location of the A-Text, where it is found preceding scene 9, hence immediately and inappropriately preceding another scene of "clowns." Placed here it is the appropriate counterpoint to the scene of Faustus and his books. The relocation is suggested by the editors of *Doctor Faustus and Other Plays*, David Bevington & Eric Rasmussen (ed.), Oxford University Press: Oxford, 1995.

[b] Ostler = horse-keeper

Robin Keep out, keep out, or else you are blown up;
you are dismembered *Ralph*, keep out, for I am about a
roaring piece of work.

Ralph Come, what dost thou with that same book?
Thou canst not read.

Robin Yes, my master and mistress shall find that I can
read, he for his forehead, she for her private study; she's
borne to bear with me, or else my art fails.

Ralph Why , *Robin*, what book is that?

Robin What book? Why, the most intolerable book for
conjuring that ere was invented by any brimstone devil.

Ralph Canst thou conjure with it?

Robin I can do all these things easily with it: first, I can
make thee drunk with ipocras[a] at any tavern in Europe

---

[a] ipocras = a wine that is sweetened with sugar; white *hippocras*
in the Venetian drinking glass in this photograph is served with a
variety of sweetmeats or 'banquetting stuffes'. The wafers and
comfits were the original accompaniments to the drink in the
context of the medieval void. During the sixteenth century these
were augmented by a vast range of new sugar-based luxury foods.
One of the rarest spices used in the production of hippocras was
carpobalsamum, the aromatic flower buds of the Balsam of Judea
Tree. In the eighteenth century a grove of the trees grew in the

for nothing; that's one of my conjuring works

Ralph Our Master Parson says that's nothing.

Robin True, *Ralph*, and more *Ralph*; if thou hast any mind to *Nan Spit*, our kitchen maid, then turn her and wind her to thy own use, as often as thou wilt, and at midnight.

Ralph O brave *Robin*, shall I have Nan Spit, and to mine own use? On that condition I'll feed thy devil with horse-bread[a] as long as he lives, of free cost.

Robin No more, sweet *Ralph*, let's go and make clean our boots, which lie foul upon our hands, and then to our conjuring in the devil's name.

Exeunt.

---

gardens belonging to the Sultan of Cairo. A late seventeenth century recipes for hippocras contains *carpobalsamum*. Musk seeds, another Egyptian spice, were also used to scent hippocras, though the most popular perfuming ingredients for the beverage were the animal products musk and ambergris.

[a] "horse-bread" = like "cow pies"

Faustus When I behold the heavens, then I repent

And curse thee wicked *Mephistophilis*,

Because thou hast deprived me of those joys.

Mephistophilis Why, *Faustus*,

Thinkst thou heaven is such a glorious thing?

I tell thee tis not half so fair as thou,

Or any man that breathes on earth.[a]

Faustus How provest thou that?

Mephistophilis It was made for man;

therefore is man more excellent.

Faustus If it were made for man, 'twas made for me.

I will renounce this magic, and repent.

Enter *Good Angel*, and *Evil Angel*.

Good Angel Faustus, repent; Yet God will pity thee.

Evil Angel Thou art a spirit; God cannot pity thee

---

[a] The "Dignity of Man" in the Humanist philosophy is set against the Christian ideal. Pico della Mirandola, who wrote the seminal essay on the *Dignity of Man*, extolled magic and alchemy in its pages, as the means to a natural philosophy.

Faustus Who buzzeth in mine ears I am a spirit?

Be I a devil, yet God may pity me;

Ay, God will pity me, if I repent.

Evil Angel Ay, but *Faustus* never shall repent.

Exeunt. Angels

Faustus My heart's so hardened I cannot repent.

Scarce can I name salvation, faith, or heaven,

But fearful echoes thunder in mine ears

Faustus, thou art damned. Then swords and knives,

Poison, guns, halters, and envenomed steel

Are laid before me to dispatch my self,

And long ere this I should have slain my self,

Had not sweet pleasure conquered deep despair.

Have not I made blind *Homer* sing to me,

Of *Alexander's* love, and *Oenon's* death,[a]

And hath not he that built the walls of Thebes,

With ravishing sound of his melodious harp,

Made music with my *Mephistophilis*?

Why should I die then, or basely despair?

I am resolved: *Faustus* shall never repent,

Come, *Mephistophilis*, let us dispute again,

---

[a] References to ancient Greeks: Homer who is legendarily the blind author of the *Iliad* and *Odyssey*; Alexander is another name for Paris who deserted his own wife, Oenon, for Helen of Troy.

And argue of divine *astrology*,

Tell me, are there many heavens above the Moon?

Are all celestial bodies but one globe,

As is the substance of this centric earth?[a]

Mephistophilis As are the elements,

such are the spheres,

Mutually folded in each other's orb,

And, *Faustus*, all jointly move upon one axletree,

Whose terminine is termed the world's wide pole,

Nor are the names of *Saturn*, *Mars*, or *Jupiter*

Fained, but are erring stars.[b]

Faustus But tell me, have they all one motion?

Both *situ & tempore*?

Mephistophilis All jointly move from East to West in

four and twenty hours upon the poles of the world, but

differ in their motion upon the poles of the zodiac.

---

[a] The dialogue with Mephistophilis continues concerning
questions that are paralleled in the *Faustbuch*, corresponding to
Chapters 15, 18 and 20. But Marlowe invents different replies.

[b] Again, the common medieval cosmology is expressed: these
concentric spheres of heaven are the regions for various objects in
the sky. Their motion was a source of debate and a consternation
to mathematicians who wished to compute them, so long as this
medieval model was maintained. Copernicus' theory of a solar
system was thus originally advanced to aid astrology, by
improving its mathematics.

Faustus Tush, these slender trifles *Wagner* can deride;

Hath *Mephistophilis* no greater skill?

Who knows not the double motion of the planets?

The first is finished in a natural day;

The second thus: as *Saturn* in thirty years;

Jupiter in twelve;

Mars in four; the Sun, *Venus*, and Mercury in a year: the

Moon in twenty eight days.

Tush, these are freshmen's suppositions,

but tell me, hath every sphere a dominion or *intelligentia*?[a]

Mephistophilis Ay.

Faustus How many heavens or spheres are there?

Mephistophilis Nine: the seven planets, the firmament, and the imperial heaven.[b]

Faustus Well, resolve me in this question: Why have we not conjunctions, oppositions, aspects, eclipses, all at one time, but in some years we have more, in some less?

Mephistophilis *Per inaequalem motum respectu totius.*[c]

---

[a] Having *intellegentia* in this context is the same as being a "spirit."

[b] The *firmament* is the sphere of the stars. The *imperial heaven* is the sphere of God.

[c] "Because of unequal motion with respect to the whole." (trans. from Latin) This is the pat answer to the problem that could not be

48

Faustus Well, I am answered. Tell me who made the world?

Mephistophilis I will not.

Faustus Sweet *Mephistophilis*, tell me.

Mephistophilis Move me not, for I will not tell thee.

Faustus Villain, have I not bound thee to tell me any thing?

Mephistophilis I, that is not against our kingdom, but this is.

Think thou on hell, *Faustus*, for thou art damned.

Faustus Think *Faustus* upon God that made the world.

Mephistophilis Remember this.

Holding the signed contract

Exit.

---

answered by medieval conception of an earth-centered universe. The controversy was entertained by the School of the Night, that group of intellectuals led by Sir Walter Raleigh, to which Marlowe may have belonged and which, it is said, heard the lectures of Giordano Bruno, an Italian heretic on this matter (and other matters) whom the Church burned at the stake in 1600. But while there was presumably more tolerance in England for this heresy, Marlowe expressly avoids it, though Faustus seems to be a likely proponent. Is it irony that the Devil expounds the traditional cosmology, instead of the heresy?

Faustus Ay, go accursed spirit to ugly hell,

'Tis thou hast damned distressed *Faustus'* soul.

Is't not too late?

> Enter *Good Angel* and *Evil Angel*.

Evil Angel Too late.

Good Angel Never too late, if *Faustus* can repent.

Evil Angel If thou repent, devils shall tear thee in pieces.

Good Angel Repent, and they shall never raze thy skin.

Exeunt Angels

Faustus Ah, Christ my Savior, seek to save distressed Faustus's soul.

> Enter *Lucifer*, *Beelzebub*, and *Mephistophilis*.[a]

Lucifer Christ cannot save thy soul, for he is just;

There's none but I have interest in the same.

Faustus O, who art thou that look'st so terrible?

---

[a] Lucifer also appears dramatically in the *Faustbuch* in Chapter 19, in order to intimidate the wavering Faustus.

Lucifer I am *Lucifer*, and this is my companion prince in hell.

Faustus O, *Faustus*! They are come to fetch away thy soul.

Lucifer We come to tell thee thou dost injure us;
Thou talkst of Christ, contrary to thy promise.
Thou shouldst not think of God: think of the devil,
And of his dame too. [a]

Faustus Nor will I henceforth: pardon me in this,
And *Faustus* vows never to look to heaven,
Never to name God, or to pray to him,
To burn his scriptures, slay his Ministers,
And make my spirits pull his churches down.

Lucifer Do so, and we will highly gratify thee. Faustus, we are come from hell to show thee some pastime. Sit down, and thou shalt see all the Seven Deadly Sins appear in their proper shapes.

Faustus That sight will be as pleasing unto me as paradise was to *Adam*, the first day of his creation.

---

[a] "The Devil and his Dame": the *dame* is his mother; it was a common saying.

Lucifer Talk not of paradise, nor creation, but mark this show; talk of the devil, and nothing else. Come away.

Enter *The Seven Deadly Sins.*[a]

Now *Faustus*, examine them of their several names and dispositions.

Faustus What art thou, the first??

Pride I am Pride. I disdain to have any parents.

I am like to *Ovid's* flea.

I can creep into every corner of a wench;[b]

sometimes like a periwig, I sit upon her brow;

or like a fan[c] of feathers, I kiss her lips.

Indeed I do, what do I not?

But fie, what a scent is here? I'll not speak another word,

except the ground were perfumed

and covered with cloth of arras.[d]

---

[a] This parade of the Seven Deadly Sins is not contained in the *Faustbuch*. Rather, it is lifted from the English morality plays. It makes good spectacle for theater. In a Coventry version of a morality play featuring Adam and Eve, the players actually appeared nude; it was a popular annual show. Marlowe's productions were not so risque, but sexual innuendo and bawdy dress and gesture were all fair.

[b] In a poem attributed to Ovid, a flea is admired for its capacity to climb among the clothes of pretty women and on their bodies. Marlowe's first literary work was a translation of Ovid's *Elegies*.

[c] periwig = wig

[d] arras = curtain or a wall hanging, especially one of Flemish origin

52

Faustus What art thou, the second?

Cove. I am *Covetousness*, begotten of an old churl, in an old leather bag, and might I have my wish, I would desire, that this house, and all the people in it were turned to gold, that I might lock you up in my good chest. O, my sweet gold!

Faustus What art thou, the third ?

Wrath I am *Wrath*. I had neither father nor mother.
I leapt out of a lion's mouth
when I was scarce half an hour
old, and ever since I have run up and down the world
with this case of rapiers wounding my self,
when I had no body to fight withal.
I was borne in hell, and look to it,
For some of you shall be my father.

Faustus What art thou, the fourth?

Envy I am *Envy* begotten of a Chimney-sweeper
And an Oyster wife. I cannot read,
and therefore wish all books were burnt.
I am lean with seeing others eat. O, that
there would come a famine through all the world,
that all might die, and I live alone;
then thou should'st see how fat I would be.

But must thou sit and I stand?

Come down with a vengeance.

Faustus Away envious rascal. What art thou, the fifth?

Glut. Who, I, sir? I am *Gluttony*.

My parents are all dead,

and the devil a penny they have left me,

but a bare pension,

and that is thirty meals a day and ten bevers,

a small[a] trifle to suffice nature.

O, I come of a royal parentage!

My grandfather was a gammon of bacon,

my grandmother a[b] hogs head of Claret-wine.

My godfathers were these:

Peter Pickle-herring, and Martin Martlemas-beef.

O, but my godmother, she was a jolly gentlewoman,

and well-beloved in every good town and City;

her name was mistress Margery March-beer.

Now, *Faustus*, thou hast heard all my

progeny, wilt thou bid me to supper?[c]

Faustus No, I'll see thee hanged; thou wilt eat up all my

victuals.

---

[a] bevers = snacks

[b] gammon = side of bacon

[c] A series of folk names for various foods, straight from the streets
of London. Claret was the cheapest wine and plentiful.

54

Glut. Then the devil choke thee.

Faustus Choke thyself, glutton!
What art thou, the sixth?

Sloth. I am sloth. I was begotten on a sunny bank,
where I have lain ever since,
and you have done me great
injury to bring me from thence.
Let me be carried thither again
by Gluttony and Lechery.
I'll not speak another word for a king's ransom.

Faustus What are you, Mistress Minks,
the seventh and last?

Lechery Who, I, sir?
I am one that loves an inch of raw
Mutton better then an ell of fried stock-fish,
and the first[a] letter of my name begins with lechery.

Lucifer Away, to hell, to hell.

Exeunt the Sins.

---

[a] Mutton = a slang term for a whore; ell = a unit of measure, 45
inches; *stock-fish* is dried cod and is a slang joke for an impotent
man. So the sense of this is that Lechery prefers sex above all.

Now, *Faustus,* how dost thou like this?

Faustus O, this feeds my soul.

Lucifer Tut, *Faustus,* in hell is all manner of delight.

Faustus O, might I see hell,
and return again, how happy were I then.

Lucifer Thou shalt;
I will send for thee at midnight. In meantime,
take this book, peruse it thoroughly, and thou shalt turn
thyself into what shape thou wilt.

Faustus Great thanks, mighty *Lucifer.* This will I keep as
chary as my life.

Lucifer Farewell, *Faustus,* and think on the devil.

Faustus Farewell, great *Lucifer.* Come *Mephistophilis.*

Exeunt omnes.

Enter *Wagner* solus.[b]

Wagner Learned *Faustus*,

To know the secrets of astronomy,

Graven in the book of *Jove's* high firmament,

Did mount himself to scale *Olympus* top,

Being seated in a chariot burning bright,

Drawn by the strength of yoky dragons' necks.[c]

He now is gone to prove cosmography,[d]

And, as I guess, will first arrive at Rome,

To see the *Pope*, and manner of his court,

And take some part of holy *Peter's* feast,[e]

That to this day is highly solemnized.

Exit *Wagner*

Enter *Faustus* and *Mephistophilis.*

Faustus Having now, my good *Mephistophilis*,

Past with delight the stately town of Trier,

---

[a] This scene is set forth in Chapter 22 of the *Faustbuch*, following its motifs fairly exactly.

[b] Wagner takes the role of the Chorus here, introducing the scene to follow.

[c] Yoky = joined by a yoke

[d] "…to prove cosmography" means to see if the maps of the world are correct.

[e] The Feast of St. Peter is June 25th.

Environed round with airy mountain tops,

With walls of flint, and deep entrenched lakes,

Not to be won by any conquering prince,

From *Paris* next coasting the realm of France,

We saw the river Maine fall into Rhine,

Whose banks are set with groves of fruitful vines.

Then up to Naples, rich Campania,

Whose buildings faire and gorgeous to the eye,

The streets straight forth, and paved with finest brick,

Quarter the town in four equivalents.

There saw we learned *Maro's* golden tomb,[a]

The way he cut an English mile in length,

Thorough a rock of stone in one night's space.

From thence to *Venice*, *Padua*, and the rest,

In midst of which a sumptuous temple stands,

That threats the stars with her aspiring top.

Thus hitherto hath *Faustus* spent his time,

But tell me now, what resting place is this?

Hast thou as erst I did command,

Conducted me within the walls of Rome?

---

[a] Maro is a name for Virgil, the Latin poet, who is reputed to have employed magic to carve a passage through a mountain. In the *Faustbuch* a similar reference is made in Chapter 22 where a world tour by Faustus is described at length: "… there saw he the Tombe of *Virgil*; & the high way that bee cutte through that mighty hill of stone in one night, the whole length of an English mile."

Mephistophilis Faustus, I have, and because we will

not be unprovided, I have taken up his

Holiness' privy-chamber for our use.

Faustus I hope his Holiness will bid us welcome.

Mephistophilis Tut, 'tis no matter man,

we'll be bold with his good cheer.

And now, my *Faustus*, that thou may'st perceive

What *Rome* containeth to delight thee with,

Know that this city stands upon seven hills

That underprop the groundwork of the same.

 [Just through the midst runs flowing Tiber's stream,

With winding banks that cut it in two parts:][a]

Over the which four stately bridges lean,

That makes safe passage to each part of Rome.

Upon the bridge called Ponto Angelo,

Erected is a castle passing strong,

Within whose walls such store of ordinance are,

And double canons, framed of carved brass,

As match the days within one complete year,

Besides the gates and high pyramids,

Which Julius Caesar brought from Africa.

---

[a] Two lines are added from the B-Text for clarity. It is the convention of all editors to insert such evident omissions to the A-Text. The fact of such corrections as these would argue for the primacy of the B-Text, although the A-Text predates it by twelve years.

Faustus Now by the kingdoms of infernal rule,

Of *Styx*, *Acheron*, and the fiery lake

Of ever-burning *Phlegiton* I swear,[a]

That I do long to see the monuments

And situation of bright splendant Rome.

Come therefore, let's away.

Mephistophilis Nay, *Faustus*, stay;

I know you'd fain see the *Pope*,

And take some part of holy *Peter's* feast,

Where thou shalt see a troupe of bald-pate friars,

Whose *summum bonum* is in belly-cheer.[b]

Faustus Well, I am content,

to compass then some sport,

And by their folly make us merriment.

Then charm me that I may be invisible, to do what I

please unseen of any whilst I stay in Rome.

Mephistophilis So, *Faustus*, now do what thou wilt,

thou shalt not be discerned.

---

[a] *Styx*, *Acheron* and *Phlegiton* are rivers of Hell.

[b] "Greatest good" (trans. from Latin); the fun made of the
Catholic authorities is popular in Elizabethan England. For this
part of the "heresy" of Faustus at least, there was much sympathy.
The scene is taken from *Faustbuch* and so presumably was
popular in Protestant Germany as well.

Sound a sennet.[a]

Enter the *Pope* and the *Cardinal of Lorrain*
to the banquet, with *Friars* attending.

Pope My Lord of *Lorraine*, wilt please you draw near.

Faustus Fall to, and the devil choke you an you spare.

Pope How now! Who's that which spoke? Friars, look
about.

Friar Here's nobody if it like your Holiness.

Pope My Lord, here is a dainty dish was sent me from
the Bishop of Milan.

Faustus I thank you sir.
Snatches it.

Pope. How now! Who's that which snatched the meat
from me? Will no man look? My Lord, this dish was
sent me from the Cardinal of Florence.

Faustus You say true; I'll ha't.
Snatches it.

---

[a] A *sennet* was a set of notes by a trumpet or cornet, like a
flourish; on stage it was to signify an actor's entrance; here it is
used mocklingly

Pope. What again? My Lord, I'll drink to your grace.

Faustus I'll pledge your grace.

Snatches his cup.

Lor. My Lord, it may be some ghost newly crept out of purgatory, come to beg a pardon of your Holiness.

Pope It may be so. Friars, prepare a dirge to lay the fury of this ghost. Once again, my lord, fall to.

The Pope crosseth himself.

Faustus What, are you crossing of your self?
Well, use that trick no more, I would advise you.

The Pope crosses himself again.

Faustus Well, there's the second time, aware the third,
I give you fair warning.

The Pope crosses himself again,
and Faustus hits him a box of the ear;
and they all run away

Faustus Come on, Mephistophilis, what shall we do?

Mephistophilis Nay, I know not. We shall be cursed

with bell, book, and candle.[a]

Faustus How?

Bell, book, and candle,

Candle, book, and bell,

Forward and backward, to curse Faustus to hell.

Anon you shall hear a hog grunt, a calf bleat, and an

ass bray, because it is Saint Peter's holy day.

Enter all the Friars to sing the Dirge.[b]

Friar. Come, brethren, let's about our business

with good devotion.

They sing.

Cursed be he that stole away his Holiness' meat

from the table.

Maledicat Dominus.[c]

Cursed be he that struck his Holiness a blow on the face.

---

[a] A ceremony of exorcism. Nowadays, the term "bell, book and
candle" connotes a ceremony of black magic. But in those days
magic might be practiced either for God or against Him.
Employment of holy "white magic" was legendary of many
Saints. St. Peter defeated Simon Magus by magic, causing him to
fall to death after he had taken flight magically. Simon Magus,
who called himself Faustus (or "the chosen one" in Latin), took a
whore to be his mistress, calling her Helen, after Helen of Troy,
whom he claimed she must be by reincarnation.

[b] Dirge = a lament for the dead, especially one forming part of a
funeral rite.

[c] "May the Lord curse him." (trans. from Latin)

Maledicat Dominus.

Cursed be he that took Friar Sandelo a blow on the pate.

Maledicat Dominus.

Cursed be he that disturbeth our holy Dirge.

Maledicat Dominus.

Cursed be he that took away his Holiness' wine.

Maledicat Dominus.

Et omnes sancti. Amen.

> *Faustus* and *Mephistophilis* beat the Friars,
>
> and fling fireworks among them; and so exeunt.

.... **Scene 9** ....

> Enter *Robin* and *Ralph* with a silver goblet.

Robin Come, *Ralph*, did not I tell thee we were for ever made by this doctor *Faustus'* book? *Ecce signum*, here's aᵃ simple purchase for horse-keepers: our horses shall eat no hay as long as this lasts.

> *Enter the Vintner.*

Ralph But *Robin*, here comes the vintner.

ᵃ "Behold a sign…" (trans. from Latin)

Robin Hush, I'll gull him supernaturally. Drawer, I hope all is paid; God be with you. Come, *Ralph*.

Vintner Soft, sir, a word with you. I must yet have a goblet paid from you ere you go.

Robin I, a goblet, *Ralph*; I, a goblet? I scorn you, and you are but a [********]. I, a goblet? Search me.[a]

Vintner I mean so, sir, with your favor.

Robin How say you now?

Vintner I must say somewhat to your fellow. You, sir.

Ralph Me, sir. Me, sir. Search your fill. Now, sir, you may be ashamed to burden honest men with a matter of truth.

Vintner Well, tone of you hath this goblet about you.

Ro. You lie, Drawer; 'tis afore me. Sirrah you, I'll teach ye to impeach honest men; stand by; I'll scour you for a goblet. Stand aside you had best, I charge you in the

---

[a] The absent phrasing is space for any obscenity to be supplied at will by the individual actor.

name of Beelzebub. Look to the goblet ,

Aside to Ralph

Vintner What mean you, sirrah?

Robin I'll tell you what I mean.
He reads from a book.

Sanctobulorum Periphrasticon -- Nay, I'll tickle you , Vintner.

Look to the goblet, Ralph.
Aside to Ralph.

*Polypragmos Belseborams framanto pacostiphos tostu,
Mephistophilis, &c.* [a]

Enter *Mephistophilis*,
sets squibs at their backs
[and then exit];[b] they run about.

Vintner *O nomine Domini*, what mean'st thou, *Robin*?
Thou[c] hast no goblet.

---

[a] The words are gibberish, but sound like Latin. Again the actor might extend it for effect, according to his own invention. The nonsense incantation succeeds nonetheless to invoke Mephistophilis.

[b] squib = a small firecracker, or a firecracker that spews fire but does not explode

[c] "In the name of God." (trans. from Latin)

Ralph *Peccatum peccatorum.* Here's thy goblet, good Vintner.[a]

Robin *Misericordia pro nobis.* What shall I do? Good devil,[b] forgive me now, and I'll never rob thy library more.

Enter to them *Mephistophilis.*

Meph. Vanish villains, th'one like an ape, another like a bear, the third an ass, for doing this enterprise.
Monarch of hell, under whose black survey
Great potentates do kneel with awful fear,
Upon whose altars thousand souls do lie,
How am I vexed with these villains charms?
From Constantinople am I hither come,
Only for pleasure of these damned slaves.

Robin How, from Constantinople?
You have had a great journey.
Will you take six pence in your purse to pay for your supper, and be gone?

Mephistophilis Well villains, for your presumption,
I transform thee into an ape, and thee into a dog,

---

[a] "Sin of sins." (trans. from Latin)
[b] "Mercy on us." (trans. from Latin)

and so be gone.

Exit.

Rob. How, into an ape? That's brave. I'll have fine sport with the boys. I'll get nuts and apples enough.

Ralph And I must be a dog.

Exeunt.

Robin I'faith thy head will never be out of the pottage pot.

.... **Scene 10** ....ᵃ

Enter *Chorus.*ᵇ

Chorus When Faustus had with pleasure ta'en the view

———————————————

ᵃ The scene borrows from episodes in the *Faustbuch*, corresponding to Chapter 29. The Emperor in Marlowe's text is Carlos the Fifth of Spain; he was Holy Roman emperor (1519-1558) and king of Spain as Charles I (1516-1556). He summoned the Diet of Worms (1521) which took up the matter of Martin Luther and ended in the declaration that Luther was an outlaw. Later, under his auspices, the Council of Trent met (1545-1563) and established the principles of the Counter-Reformation.
The scene differs between the A-Text and the B-Text where it is much extended.

ᵇ This chorus is relocated from its original place in the A-Text, immediately succeeding the Scene 8, with the Pope, because it introduces the following scene with the Emperor.

Of rarest things, and royal courts of kings,

He stayed his course, and so returned home,

Where such as bear his absence, but with grief,

I mean his friends and nearest companions,

Did gratulate his safety with kind words,

And in their conference of what befell,

Touching his journey through the world and air,

They put forth questions of astrology,

Which *Faustus* answered with such learned skill,

As they admired and wondered at his wit.

Now is his fame spread forth in every land;

Amongst the rest the Emperor is one,

Carolus the fifth, at whose palace now

Faustus is feasted 'mongst his noblemen.

What there he did in trial of his art,

I leave untold-- your eyes shall see perform'd.

Enter *Emperor*, *Faustus*,
and a *Knight*, with attendants.

Emperor Master Doctor *Faustus*,

I have heard strange report of thy knowledge

in the black art, how that none in

my Empire, nor in the whole world

can compare with thee,

for the rare effects of magic;

they say thou hast a familiar

spirit, by whom thou canst

accomplish what thou list. This,

therefore, is my request, that thou

let me see some proof of thy

skill, that mine eyes may be

witnesses to confirm what mine

ears have heard reported, and

here I swear to thee, by the

honor of mine imperial crown,

that whatever thou doest,

thou shalt be no ways prejudiced or endamaged.

Knight I'faith he looks much like a conjuror.

   Aside

Faustus My gracious sovereign, though I must confess

myself far inferior to the report men have published,

and nothing answerable to the honor of your imperial

majesty, yet for that love and duty binds me thereunto,

I am content to do whatsoever your majesty shall

command me.

Emperor Then, Doctor Faustus,

mark what I shall say. As

I was sometime solitary set within my closet, sundry

thoughts arose about the honour of mine ancestors, how

they had won by prowess such exploits, got such riches,

subdued so many kingdoms,

as we that do succeed, or they

that shall hereafter possess our throne,

shall (I fear me) never attain to that degree of high

  renown and great authority,

amongst which kings is Alexander the Great, chief[a]

spectacle of the world's preeminence,

The bright shining of whose glorious acts

Lightens the world with his reflecting beams,

As when I hear but motion made of him,

It grieves my soul I never saw the man.

If, therefore, thou, by cunning of thine art,

Canst raise this man from hollow vaults below,

Where lies entombed this famous conquerour,

And bring with him his beauteous paramour,

Both in their right shapes, gesture, and attire

They used to wear during their time of life,

Thou shalt both satisfy my just desire,

And give me cause to praise thee whilst I live.

Faustus My gracious Lord,

I am ready to accomplish your

request, so far forth as by art and

power of my spirit I am able to perform.

Knight I'faith that's just nothing at all.

　　　Aside

---

[a] Alexander the Great (356-323 BC), the Greek king, who it is
said conquered the known world, as far east as India. He wedded
his enemy's daughter, Roxanne.

Faustus But if it like your Grace,

it is not in my ability to present before

your eyes the true substantial bodies of those

two deceased princes, which long

since are consumed to dust.

Knight

Ay, marry, Master Doctor, now there's a sign of grace

in you, when you will confess the truth.

Aside

Faustus But such spirits as can lively resemble

Alexander and his Paramour, shall appear before your

Grace, in that manner that they best lived in,

in their most flourishing estate,

which I doubt not shall sufficiently

content your imperial majesty.

Em Go to, Master Doctor, let me see them presently.

Knight Do you hear, Master Doctor? You bring

Alexander and his paramour before the Emperor?

Faustus How then, sir?

72

Kn. I'faith that's as true as Diana turned me to a stag.[a]

Faustus No, sir, but when Acteon died,

he left the horns for you. Mephistophilis, be gone.

Exit *Mephistophilis.*

Kn. Nay, an you go to conjuring, I'll be gone.

Exit *Knight.*

Faustus I'll meet with you anon for interrupting me so.

Here they are my gracious Lord.

Enter *Mephistophilis*
with Alexander and his paramour.

Emperor Master Doctor, I heard this Lady while she

Lived had a wart or mole in her neck.

How shall I know whether[b] it be so or no?

---

[a] Diana (Artemis in Greek) is an ancient mythological figure, an immortal goddess, who is protector of nymphs and wilderness. Seen bathing by Acteon, she turned him into a stag, lest he boast about seeing her naked. Then she turned her hounds upon him, who drove him to ground and killed him.

[b] In the original German version of the *Faustbuch*, the mole or wart is on her "backside" and so for proof she displays it to the Emperor. Marlowe's version in English omitted this and a number of other bawdy bits and added for good measure some additional moralizing.

Faustus Your highness may boldly go and see.

Exit Alexander.

Emperor Sure these are no spirits, but the true

Substantial bodies of those two deceased princes.

Faustus Will't please your highness now to

send for the knight that was so pleasant

with me here of late?

Emperor One of you call him forth.

Exit *Attendant.*

Enter the *Knight* with a pair of horns on his head.[a]

Emperor How now, sir knight?

Why I had thought thou hadst been a bachelor,

but now I see thou hast a wife, that not only gives thee

horns, but makes thee wear them, feel[b] on thy head.

Knight Thou damned wretch, and execrable dog,

Bred in the concave of some monstrous rock.

How darest thou thus abuse a gentleman?

---

[a] The episode corresponds to *Faustbuch* in Chapter 30.

[b] The man whose wife cheats on him is a "cuckold" in the old parlance, and he is represented in folklore as a man with horns on his head.

Villain, I say, undo what thou hast done.

Faustus O, not so fast sir; there's no haste; but, good,
are you remembered how you crossed me in my
conference with the Emperor?
I think I have met with you for it.

Emperor Good Master Doctor,
at my entreaty release him;
he hath done penance sufficient.

Faustus My Gracious Lord,
not so much for the injury he
offered me here in your presence,
as to delight you with some
mirth, hath Faustus worthily
requited this injurious knight,
which being all I desire,
I am content to release him of his
horns: and, sir knight, hereafter speak well of scholars.
Mephistophilis, transform him straight.
Mephistophilis removes the horns.
Now my good Lord having done my duty,
I humbly take my leave.

Emp. Farewell, Master Doctor, yet ere you go, expect
from me a bounteous reward.

Exit Emperor.

Faustus Now, Mephistophilis,
the restless course that time
doth run with calm and silent foot,
Shortening my days and thread of vital life,
Calls for the payment of my latest years.
Therefore, sweet Mephistophilis,
let us make haste to Wertenberg.

Mephistophilis What, will you go on horse back, or on
foot?

Faustus Nay, 'til I am past this faire
and pleasant green, I'll walk on foot.

.... **Scene 11** ....ᵃ

Enter a Horse-courser.

Horse-courser I have been all this day seeking one
master Fustian: mass, see where he is. ᵇ
God save you, Master Doctor.

ᵃ Again, the scene is derived from an episode in the *Faustbuch*,
corresponding to Chapter 34.

ᵇ The phrase "master Fustian" is a play on the word Faust. A
"fustian" is a pompous fellow, prone to bombast.

Faustus What, horse-courser; you are well met.

Horse-courser Do you hear sir?
I have brought you forty dollars for your horse.

Faustus I cannot sell him so.
If thou lik'st him for fifty, take him.

Horse-courser Alas sir, I have no more;
I pray you speak for me.

Mephistophilis I pray you let him have him;
he is an honest fellow,
and he has a great charge, neither wife nor child.

Faustus Well, come give me your money.
My boy will deliver him to you,
but I must tell you one thing before you have
him: ride him not into the water at any hand.

Horse-courser Why sir, will he not drink of all waters?

Faustus O yes, he will drink of all waters,
but ride him not
into the water: ride him over hedge or ditch,
or where thou wilt, but not into the water.

Horse-courser Well, sir—

Now am I made man forever. I'll not

leave my horse for forty.

If he had but the quality of hey-ding-ding,

  Aside.

hey-ding-ding, I'd make a brave living on him;

he has a buttock so slick as an eel.[a]

Well, God b' wi' ye sir; your boy will deliver him me.

But hark ye, sir, if my horse be sick, or

ill at ease, if I bring his water to you, you'll tell me what
is?[b]

Exit Horse-courser

Faustus Away, you villain;

what, dost think I am a horse-doctor?

What art thou, Faustus, but a man condemned to die?

Thy fatal time doth draw to final end;

Despair doth drive distrust unto my thoughts:

Confound these passions with a quiet sleep.

Tush, Christ did call the thief upon the cross,

Then rest thee, Faustus, quiet in conceit.[c]

  Sleeps in his chair.

---

[a] The phrase "hey-ding-ding" is used in bawdy songs, meant in
the same manner as "nookie." He thinks that if the horse could be
employed in stud, he might make a good living from him.

[b] "Bring him water…" meaning bring his urine.

[c] conceit = knowledge

Enter Horse-courser all wet, crying.

Horse-courser Alas, alas!
Doctor Fustian, quotha? Mass, Doctor
Lopus was never such a Doctor.
Has given me a purgation[a]
has purged me of forty dollars;
I shall never see them more.
But yet, like an ass as I was,
I would not be ruled by him,
for he bade me I should ride him into no water.
Now I, thinking my horse had had
some rare quality that he would not
have had me known of, I, l
ike a venturous youth, rid him into the
deep pond at the town's end. I was no sooner in the
middle of the pond, but my horse vanished away,
and I sat upon a bottle of hey,
never so near drowning in my life. But[b]
I'll seek out my Doctor, and have my forty dollars again,
or I'll make it the dearest horse.
O, yonder is his snipper-
snapper, do you hear?

---

[a] Doctor Lopus is Dr. Lopez, personal physician to Queen
Elizabeth. He was hanged in 1594 for attempting to poison her.
[b] bottle of hey = bundle of hay

You, hey-pass, where's your[a] master?

Mephistophilis Why sir, what would you?
You cannot speak with him.

Horse-courser But I will speak with him.

Mephistophilis Why, he's fast asleep;
come some other time.

Horse-courser I'll speak with him now,
or I'll break his glass-windows about his ears.

Mephistophilis I tell thee
he has not slept this eight nights.

Horse-courser And he have not slept
this eight weeks, I'll speak with him.

Mephistophilis See where he is fast asleep.

Horse-courser Ay, this is he;
God save ye Master Doctor, Master
Doctor, Master Doctor Fustian,
forty dollars, forty dollars for a bottle of hey.

Mephistophilis Why, thou seest he hears thee not.

Horse-courser So, ho, ho; so, ho, ho.

Hollers in his ear.

No, will you not wake? I'll make you wake ere I go.

Pulls Faustus by the leg, and pulls it away.[a]

Alas, I am undone! What shall I do?

Faustus O, my leg, my leg, help Mephistophilis, call the officers, my leg, my leg.

Mephistophilis Come, villain, to the Constable.

Horse-courser O Lord sir, let me go, and I'll give you forty dollars more.

Mephistophilis Where be they?

Horse-courser I have none about me. Come to my ostry, and I'll[b] give them you.

---

[a] In the *Faustbuch* this leg-pulling prank is a separate incident, involving a Jew who had lent Faust money and to whom he had given his leg for surety. But then when Faustus wished to repay the debt, the leg had been discarded and could not be returned, so Faustus owed him nothing.

[b] ostry = horse stable

Mephistophilis Be gone quickly.

Horse-courser runs away.

Faustus What, is he gone? Farewell he.[a]
Faustus has his leg again.

And the Horse-courser I take it, a bottle of hey for his labour. Well, this trick shall cost him forty dollars more.

Enter *Wagner.*

How now, Wagner; what's the news with thee?

Wagner Sir, the Duke of Vanholt doth earnestly entreat your company.

Faustus The Duke of Vanholt! an honourable gentleman, to whom I must be no niggard of my cunning. Come, Mephistophilis, let's away to him. Exeunt.

---

[a] As to say, "good riddance."

Enter to them the *Duke of Vanholt*
and the *Duchess*; the *Duke* speaks.

Duke Believe me, Master Doctor, this merriment hath
much pleased me.

Faustus My gracious lord, I am glad it contents you so
well. But it may be, madam, you take no delight in this; I
have heard that great bellied women do long for some [b]
dainties or other. What is it, madam?
Tell me, and you shall have it.

Dutch. Thanks, good Master Doctor,
And for I see your courteous intent to pleasure me,
I will not hide from you the thing my heart desires,
and were it now summer, as it is January, and the dead
time of the winter, I would desire no better meat
then a dish of ripe grapes.

---

[a] Another episode from the *Faustbuch*, corresponding to Chapter 39. In this instance, the text is in some particulars exactly imitated. In this and in other scenes, it may be suspected that Marlowe (or some other unknown author) may have inserted these to fatten the entertainment. Since the Faustbuch is comprised of such anecdotal episodes, it would be natural and easy to incorporate such ones as one wanted at will. No copyrights inhibited any one from so doing, or even from publishing another person's works.

[b] great bellied ladies = pregnant ladies

Faustus Alas, madam, that's nothing.
Mephistophilis, be gone:

      Exit *Mephistophilis.*

Were it a greater thing than this, so
it would content you, you should have it.

      Enter *Mephistophilis* with the grapes.

Here they be, madam; wil't please you taste on them.

Duke Believe me, Master Doctor,
this makes me wonder above the rest,
that being in the dead time of winter, and in
the month of January,
how you should come by these grapes.

Faustus If it like your Grace,
the year is divided into two
circles over the whole world,
that when it is here winter
with us, in the contrary circle it is summer with them,
as in *India*, *Saba*, and farther countries in the East;
and by means of a swift spirit that I have,
I had them brought hither, as ye

see, how do you like them madam? Be they good?[a]

Dut. Believe me, Master Doctor, they be the best grapes
that e'er I tasted in my life before.

Faustus I am glad they content you so, madam.

Duke Come, madam, let us in, where you must
well reward this learned man for the great kindness
he hath showed to you.

Dut. And so I will my Lord, and whilst I live,
rest beholding for this courtesy.

Faustus I humbly thank your Grace.

Duke Come, Master Doctor,
follow us and receive your reward.

Exeunt.

---

[a] In *Faustbuch*, it reads almost identically: "Doctor *Faustus* tolde
him, may it please your Grace to vnderstand, that the yere is
deuided into two circles ouer the whole world, that when with vs
it is Winter, in the contrary circle it is notwithstanding Sommer,
for in *India* and *Saba* there falleth or setteth the Sunne, so that it is
so warme, that they haue twise a yeare fruite: and gracious Lorde,
I haue a swift Spirit, the which can in the twinckling of an eye
fulfill my desire in any thing, wherefore I sent him into those
Countries, who hath brought this fruite as you see: whereat the
Duke was in great admiration."

Enter *Wagner*, solus.

Wagner I think my master means to die shortly,

For he hath given to me all his goods,

And yet me thinks, if that death were near,

He would not banquet, and carouse, and swill

Amongst the students, as even now he doth,

Who are at supper with such belly-cheer,

As Wagner never beheld in all his life.

See where they come. Belike the feast is ended.

Enter *Faustus*, with two or three *Scholars*[b]

Scholars Master Doctor Faustus, since our conference

about faire ladies, which was the beautiful'st in all the

world, we have determined with our selves, that Helen of

Greece was the admirabl'st Lady that ever lived.

Therefore, Master Doctor, if you will do us that favor,

---

[a] The conjure of Helen is also contained in the *Faustbuch*; there
she becomes his mistress and even bears him a child. The old man
who visits Faustus in this scene to urge him to repent is paralleled
also in the *Faustbuch*, wherein the old man is a neighbor who had
witnessed these evil goings-on for years (yet had not reported it to
the authorities as the crime of witchcraft). For by that time in
Germany persons were charged and punished for the crime of
witchcraft, very often upon the reports of neighbors. Otherwise,
this episode of the old man is the Christian motif of an interceding
saint or hermit, such as saved Lancelot on his quest for the Holy
Grail, etc.

[b] "scholars" = students

as to let us see that peerless Dame of Greece,

whom all the world admires for majesty,

we should think our selves much beholding unto you.

Faustus Gentlemen, for that I know your

friendship is unfained, and Faustus custom is not to deny

the just requests of those that wish him well,

you shall behold that peerless dame of Greece, no

otherwise for pomp and majesty, then

when sir Paris crossed the seas with her and

brought the spoils to rich Dardania.

Be silent then, for danger is in words.[a]

Music sounds, and Helen passeth over the stage.

Scholar Too simple is my wit to tell her praise,

Whom all the world admires for majesty.

Scholar No marvel though the angry Greeks pursued

With ten years war the rape of such a queen,

Whose heavenly beauty passeth all compare.

Scholar Since we have seen the pride of nature's

---

[a] Dardania = the land of Troy. Marlowe presumes that the audience knows the story of the *Iliad*; it had been recently (and for the first time) translated to English and published. In all of his dramas Marlowe freely used such allusions to classical literature. It was in part an imitation of that literature. It was in part the intellectual convention of an educated man.

works, And only paragon of excellence.

Enter an *Old Man*.

Let us depart, and for this glorious deed
Happy and blest be Faustus evermore.

Faustus Gentlemen, Farewell, the same I wish to you.

Exeunt *Scholars*.

Old Man Ah, Doctor Faustus, that I might prevail
To guide thy steps unto the way of life,
By which sweet path thou maist attain the goal
That shall conduct thee to celestial rest.
Break heart, drop blood, and mingle it with tears,
Tears falling from repentant heaviness
Of thy most vile and loathsome filthiness,
The stench whereof corrupts the inward soul
With such flagitious crimes of heinous sins,[a]
As no commiseration may expel,
But mercy, Faustus, of thy Savior sweet,
Whose blood alone must wash away thy guilt.

Faustus Where art thou, Faustus?
Wretch, what hast thou done?

---

[a] flagitious = characterized by extremely brutal or cruel crimes; vicious

88

Damned art thou, Faustus, damned, despair and die;

Hell calls for right, and with a roaring voice

Says, Faustus, come! thine hour is come.

Mephistophilis gives him a dagger.

And Faustus-- will come to do thee right.

Old Man Ah stay, good Faustus,

stay thy desperate steps.

I see an angel hovers ore thy head,

And, with a vial full of precious grace,

Offers to pour the same into thy soul;

Then call for mercy and avoid despair.

Faustus Ah, my sweet friend, I feel thy words

To comfort my distressed soul;

Leave me a while to ponder on my sins.

Old Man I go, sweet Faustus, but with heavy cheer,

Fearing the ruin of thy hopeless soul.

Faustus Accursed Faustus, where is mercy now?

I do repent, and yet I do despair.

Hell strives with grace for conquest in my breast;

What shall I do to shun the snares of death?

Mephistophilis Thou traitor, Faustus, I arrest thy soul

For disobedience to my sovereign lord,

Revolt, or I'll in piece-meal tear thy flesh.

Faustus Sweet Mephistophilis, entreat thy lord

To pardon my unjust presumption,

And with my blood again I will confirm

My former vow I made to Lucifer.

Mephistophilis Do it then quickly,

with unfeigned heart,

Lest greater danger do attend thy drift.

Faustus Torment, sweet friend,

that base and crooked age,

That dar'st dissuade me from thy Lucifer,

With greatest torments that our hell affords.

Mephistophilis His faith is great,

I cannot touch his soul,

Aside

But what I may afflict his body with,

I will attempt, which is but little worth.

Faustus One thing, good servant, let me crave of thee:

To glut the longing of my heart's desire,

That I might have unto my paramour,

That heavenly Helen which I saw of late,

Whose sweet embracings may extinguish clean

These thoughts that do dissuade me from my vow,

And keep mine oath I made to Lucifer.

Mephistophilis Faustus, this, or
what else thou shalt desire,

Shall be performed in twinkling of an eye.

Enter Helen.

Faustus Was this the face that launched
a thousand ships?

And burnt the topless towers of Ilium?ᵃ

Sweet Helen, make me immortal with a kiss.

Her lips suck forth my soul; see where it flies.

Come, Helen, come give me my soul again.

Here will I dwell, for heaven be in these lips,

And all is dross that is not Helena.

Enter *Old man*

I will be Paris, and for love of thee,

Instead of Troy shall Wertenberg be sacked,

And I will combat with weak Menelaus,

And wear thy colours on my plumed crest;

Yea, I will wound Achilles in the heel,

And then return to Helen for a kiss.

ᵃ Ilium = the Greek name for the city of Troy

O, thou art fairer than the evening air,

Clad in the beauty of a thousand stars,

Brighter art thou than flaming Jupiter,

when he appeared to hapless Semele,[a]

More lovely then the monarch of the sky

In wanton Arethusa's azured arms,[b]

And none but thou shalt be my paramour.

Exeunt All but the old man.

Old man Accursed *Faustus*, miserable man,

That from thy soul exclud'st the grace of heaven,

And fly'st the throne of his tribunal seat,

Enter the *Devils.*

Satan begins to sift me with his pride:

As in this furnace God shall try my faith,

---

[a] Jupiter (Zeus in the Greek) had many sexual liaisons; it is the character of such a God to procreate freely and live at will. Nevertheless, his wife was jealous and offended, often angry. In the case of Semele, who was a mortal woman, the conniving wife persuaded the mistress to ask Jupiter to appear to her in his full glory. Hence, as the God of Sky, Light and Thunderbolts, Jupiter's glory incinerated her.

[b] Arethusa was a nymph of the water, occupying a certain spring. She was loved by a river god, named Alpheus, who pursued her and when he caught her joined his waters to hers. In a Hellenistic variation, she first was disguised by Artemis as a cloud, and then as a fountain was finally captured, before their waters intermingled. Marlowe here mistakes his allusion, making Jupiter (Zeus) the predator. It was a pretty obscure allusion.

92

My faith, vile fuel, shall triumph over thee.

Ambitious fiends, see how the heavens smiles

At your repulse, and laughs your state to scorn.

Hence, hell! for hence I fly unto my God.

Exeunt old man.

.... **Scene 14** ....[a]

Enter *Faustus* with the *Scholars*.

Faustus Ah, gentlemen!

Scholar What ails Faustus?

Faustus Ah, my sweet chamber-fellow! Had I lived with
thee, then had I lived still, but now I die eternally. Look,
comes he not? Comes he not?

Scholar What means Faustus?

Scholar Belike he is grown into some sickness by

---

[a] This scene is pure Marlowe. While in the *Faustbuch* his students
also visit him on his last day, the dialogue here is distinctive and
the soliloquy of Faustus, counting down to the hour of his death,
is unique. Both the opening scenes and this final scene comprise
the most powerful poetry of Marlowe, in which he expresses his
view of Faustus; it is in these scenes that Marlowe seems the most
sympathetic toward Faustus, while for the rest, Faustus is
sometimes a buffoon.

being over solitary.

Scholar If it be so, we'll have physicians to cure him;
'tis but a surfeit. Never fear man.

Faustus A surfeit of deadly sin that hath damned both
body and soul.

Scholar Yet, Faustus,
look up to heaven; remember God's mercies are infinite.

Faustus But Faustus' offense can never be pardoned:
the serpent that tempted Eve may be saved,[a]
but not Faustus. Ah, gentlemen, hear me with patience,
and tremble not at my speeches, though my
heart pants and quivers to remember that
I have been a student here these
thirty years. O, would I had never seen
Wertenberg, never read book..
And what wonders I have done, all Germany
can witness, yea all the world,
for which Faustus hath lost
both Germany, and the world,
yea heaven itself, heaven the
seat of God, the throne of the blessed,
the kingdom of joy, and must remain in hell for ever,

---

[a] Actually, the serpent, as the incarnate Devil, cannot be saved.

hell, ah, hell for ever! Sweet
friends, what shall become of Faustus,
being in hell for ever?

Scholar Yet, Faustus, call on God.

Faustus On God, whom Faustus hath abjured, on God,
whom Faustus hath blasphemed. Ah, my God, I would
weep, but the devil draws in my tears. Gush forth blood
instead of tears. Yea, life and soul.
Oh, he stays my tongue.
I would lift up my hands,
but, see, they hold them, they hold them.

All Who Faustus?

Faustus Lucifer and Mephistophilis.
Ah Gentlemen! I gave them my soul for my cunning.

All God forbid.

Faustus God forbade it indeed,
but Faustus hath done it.
For vain pleasure of four and twenty years,
hath Faustus lost eternal
joy and felicity. I writ them a bill with mine one blood;
the date is expired, the time will come,
and he will fetch Mephistophilis.

Scholar. Why did not Faustus tell us of this before, that
divines might have prayed for thee?

Faustus Oft have I thought to have done so,
but the devil threatened to tear me in pieces
if I named God, to fetch both body and soul,
if I once gave ear to divinity.
And now 'tis too late.
Gentlemen, away, lest you perish with me.

Scholar O, what shall we do to Faustus?

Faustus Talk not of me,
but save yourselves, and depart.

Scholar God will strengthen me;
I will stay with Faustus.

Scholar Tempt not God, sweet friend,
but let us into the next room, and there pray for him.

Faustus Ay, pray for me, pray for me,
and what noise soever ye hear,
come not unto me, for nothing can rescue me.

Scholar Pray thou, and
we will pray that God may have mercy upon thee.

Faustus Gentlemen, farewell.

If I live 'til morning, I'll visit you,

if not, Faustus is gone to hell.

All Faustus, farewell.

Exeunt *Scholars*.

The clock strikes eleven

Faustus Ah *Faustus*,

Now hast thou but one bare hour to live,

And then thou must be damned perpetually.

Stand still you ever moving spheres of heaven,

That time may cease, and midnight never come;

Fair Nature's eye, rise, rise again, and make

Perpetual day, or let this hour be but a year,

A month, a week, a natural day,

That Faustus may repent, and save his soul.

O lente, lente, currite noctis equi.[a]

The stars move still, time runs, the clock will strike.

The devil will come, and Faustus must be damned.

O, I'll leap up to my God who pulls me down?

See, see where Christ's blood streames in the firmament;

One drop would save my soule,

half a drop, ah, my Christ!

---

[a] A quotation from Ovid's *Amores* (I, xiiii, 40): "…run slowly,
slowly, you horses of the night." In its original context, the line is
a prayer to extend the act of physical love.

97

Ah, rend not my heart for naming of my Christ,

Yet will I call on him. Oh spare me, Lucifer!

Where is it now? 'Tis gone,

And see where God stretcheth out his arm,

And bends his ireful brows.

Mountains and hills, come, come and fall on me,

And hide me from the heavy wrath of God.

No no, then will I headlong run into the earth;

Earth gape! O no, it will not harbour me.

You stars that reigned at my nativity,

Whose influence hath allotted death and hell,

Now draw up Faustus like a foggy mist,

Into the entrails of yon laboring cloud,

That when you vomit forth into the air,

My limbs may issue from your smoky mouths,

So that my soul may but ascend to heaven.

Ah, half the hour is past:

The clock strikes the half hour

'Twill all be past anon.

Oh God, if thou wilt not have mercy on my soul,

Yet for Christ's sake, whose blood hath ransomed me,

Impose some end to my incessant pain;

Let Faustus live in hell a thousand years,

A hundred thousand, and at last be saved.

O, no end is limited to damned souls.

Why wert thou not a creature wanting soul?

98

Or why is this immortal that thou hast?

Ah, Pythagoras' metempsychosis, were that true,[a]

This soul should fly from me, and I be changed

Unto some brutish beast.

All beasts are happy, for when they die,

Their souls are soon dissolved in elements,

But mine must live still to be plagued in hell.

Curst be the parents that engendered me.

No, Faustus, curse thyself, curse Lucifer,

That hath deprived thee of the joys of heaven.

The clock striketh twelve

O, it strikes, it strikes! Now, body, turn to air,

Or Lucifer will bear thee quick to hell.

   Thunder and lightning.

O soul, be changed into little water drops,

And fall into the ocean, ne'er be found.

My God, my God, look not so fierce on me;

       Enter *Devils*.

Adders, and serpents, let me breathe a while;

Ugly hell gape not, come not Lucifer;

I'll burn my books! Ah, Mephistophilis.

---

[a] Pythagorus' *metempsychoses* is understood here to be the transference of the soul from one life-form to another. In the 6th century before Christ this idea was a variation of the doctrine of reincarnation with which we are familiar from the philosophies of India.

Exeunt *Devils* with *Faustus.*

Enter *Chorus.*[a]

Cut is the branch that might have grown full straight,

And burned is Apollo's laurel bough[b]

That sometime grew within this learned man.

Faustus is gone; regard his hellish fall,

Whose fiendful fortune may exhort the wise,

Only to wonder at unlawful things,

Whose deepness doth entice such forward wits,

To practice more than heavenly power permits.

Exit.

Terminat hora diem, terminat auctor opus.[c]

---

[a] The chorus sums up the lesson, much as the author to the *Faustbuch* did, or as it would occur in a morality play, and as the chorus may have been applied in Greek and Roman drama upon which ultimately this literature is dependent.

[b] Apollo's laurel branch = the symbolic reward for triumph, given by custom in ancient Greece

[c] "The hour ends its day; the author ends his work." (trans. from Latin)

Supplemental Materials

Background—in General

Important Literature of Faust:

1. Anonymous. *Historia von D. Johann Fausten* , Frankfurt am Main: Johann Spies, 1587 (the so-called German Faustbuch)

2. *The historie of the damnable life and deserved death of Doctor John Faustus. Newly imprinted, and in convenient places imperfect matter amended: according to the true copie printed at Franckfort, and translated into English by P. F. Gent* 1592, London (the so-called English Faustbook)

3. Christopher Marlowe. *The Tragicall History of D. Faustus* (1604).

4. Gotthold Lessing. *Faust* (fragmant, 1784).

5. Adalbert von Chamisso. *Faust: Ein Versuch* (1804)

6. *Peter Schlemihls Wundersame Geschichte* (Peter Schlemihl's Miraculous Story), written in German by exiled French aristocrat Adelbert von Chamisso (1813).

7. Johann Wolfgang von Goethe. *Faust: Eine Tragšgie* (Erster Teil, 1808; Zweiter Teil, completed 1831, published 1833).

8. Christian Dietrich Grabbe. *Don Juan und Faust* (1829).

9. Nikolaus Lenau. *Faust: Ein Gedicht* (1836)

10. Woldemar Nurnberger. *Josephus Faust* (1847)

11. Heinrich Heine. *Doktor Faust: Ein Tanzpoem, nebst kuriosen Berichten Ÿber Teufel,* Hexen und Dichtkunst (1851).

12. Paul Valery. *Mon Faust* (1946).

13. Thomas Mann. *Doktor Faustus* (1950).

Selected musical works based on the Faust legend

1. Hector Berlioz. *The Damnation of Faust* (1846), a dramatic cantata based on a French version of Goethe's work by Gerard de Nerval. This composition is also staged as an opera.

2. Charles Gounod. *Faust* (1859), an opera based on part one of Goethe's work. Libretto by Jules Barbier and Michel Carr .

3. Franz Liszt. *A Faust Symphony* (1854, revised 1857-1861)

Relationship to Common Folktale Types:

1. *Master Builder Legends*, in which a mortal tricks a supernatural being (typically a troll or a giant) into helping him build a grand edifice, have much in common with the Faust stories.

2. *Devil's Bridge Legends.* In these tales (type 1191) the devil builds a bridge but is then cheated out of the human soul he expected as payment.

3. *Bearskin.* Folktales of type 361, in which a man gains a fortune and a beautiful bride by entering into a pact with the devil.

4. *The Damnable Life and Death of Stubbe Peeter* is a werewolf legend that shares many motifs with the Faust legends.

5. *Straightening a Curly Hair.* Folktales of type 1175, in which a demon helper is defeated because he cannot straighten a curly hair.

6. *Deceiving the Devil*, a folktale of type 1176, in which the devil loses control over his intended victim by failing to catch and return broken wind.

104

Portrait of a nubile Marlowe dated 1585.
Not entitled but often attributed to be his likeness.

In the upper right corner of the portrait is a Latin motto:
"That which Nourishes Me Destroys Me"

* 1564: born Christopher Marlowe in Canterbury, England

* 1585-87: served as spy for the Queen in Netherlands; published translation of Ovid's erotic verse

* 1589: published and presented his first play *Tamburlaine the Great*

* 1592: Marlowe authors *The Tragical Life and Death of Doctor Faustus*

* 30 January 1593: Marlowe's *The Massacre at Paris* performed in London; marked as a new play in Henslowe's account book. Plague again causes theatre closures

* 12 May 1593: Thomas Kyd arrested for possessing heretical writings; under torture he declares they belonged to Marlowe and further, accuses Marlowe of treason and sodomy

* 18 May 1593: Marlowe summoned from Thomas Walsingham's house in Kent to appear before the Privy Council on charge of heresy

* 20 May 1593: questioned by Privy Council and released on bail

* c.27 May 1593: Richard Baines' accusations against Marlowe delivered to the Privy Council.

* 30 May 1593 : Marlowe murdered in a house in Deptford by Ingram Frizer, witnessed by Robert Poley and Nicholas Skeres

* 28 June 1593: Frizer pardoned; ruled 'homicide in self-defence'

In Search of Christopher Marlowe, A.D. Wraight, Vangaurd Press: New York, 1965.

The book is a biography of Marlowe with literary criticism. It contains a number of analyses of contentious issues regarding Marlowe, including the controversy of his death, his arrest, mysteries of his youth and manuscripts.

Marlowe was born in Canterbury in 1564, at the time a small village of about 4000 but the residence of the Primate of England, the Cathedral of Canterbury where Thomas a Becket had been martyred. During Marlowe's youth Canterbury and its environs became a refuge of foreign protestants, especially French Huguenots who fled persecution. It is surmised that Marlowe learned French from such peoples.

Bibliography to this work includes: *The Death of Christopher Marlowe*, Hotson, 1925; *Christopher Marlowe in London*, Eccles, 1934; *Christopher Marlowe*, Boas, 1940; *The Tragicall History of Christopher Marlowe*, Bakeless, 1942; *The Muse's Darling*, Charles Norman, 1960.

Marlowe was born the same year as Shakespeare, the son of John Marlowe, a cobbler. He was the eldest in a family of girls. We do not know where or how but he must have obtained so early a grounding in reading, writing, grammar to qualify himself for a scholarship in 1578 (at age 15) to King's School in Canterbury. There he acquired fluency in Latin and Greek. Marlowe likely acquired his first library at this time: Ovid (whom both he and Shakespeare revered), Tindal's translation of the Bible, Book of Common Prayer, Works of Machiavelli, Munster's *Cosmography*. Marlowe was nicknamed Machiavel by his companions; whatever else it means, it reflects the admiration he held for the philosopher.

In 1580 (at age 17) he matriculated to Cambridge and Corpus Christi College, as the scholar of Archbishop Parker of Canterbury. A bit older (by two years) than the common scholar, he studied now Latin and Hebrew. He often read books other than prescribed, as was frowned upon. The object of his study should have been the occupation of divinity.

One elder student at Corpus Christi at the time (but one he should not have likely known while he was a freshman) was Francis Kett who some eight years later was burned at the stake for heresy. He in fact was a zealot of peculiar Christian views, who went to the fire in sack cloth and as the fire consumed him, leapt and danced, while he shouted, "Blessed Be God."

At age 23-5 (1585-7) Marlowe's scholarship was interrupted by unexplained absences from the College. It is thought that these absences are to be attributed to services to the Privy Council which subsequently wrote to the college in June 1587 to ensure his reinstatement, explaining his absences for reason of that service. That service, by other evidence, is thought to entail "spying" for the "secret service" of the Queen, spying at the Jesuit seminary in Rheims where it is thought that conspirators gathered against the Queen. It is supposed that Francis Walsingham, who was organizer of Her Majesty's spy service, was intimate with this matter. Walsingham was a witness to the Paris Massacre when some 2,000 Huguenots were slaughtered by the French. Later in 1589 Marlowe wrote a poem concerning this Massacre in Paris.

Another player in the intrigue was Robert Poley who, with Walsingham's confidence, encouraged a conspiracy of assassination by Anthony Babington. Letters exchanged between Babington and Mary Queen of Scots were intercepted by Walsingham. In September 1586 some seven conspirators, including Babington, were executed. Mary was executed in February the following year. Poley and perhaps Marlowe had played to the conspirators as sympathizers. Poley was later to be one of the three who were present at Marlowe's own murder.

By the influence of that letter Marlowe was shortly granted his M.A. but he subsequently left the college for London. His first play, *Tamburlaine the Great*, was produced just two years later.

About this time (1587) Marlowe's first literary production appeared, a translation of Ovid's *Elegies*, love poems that were particularly erotic.

Subsequently the younger cousin of Walsingham, Thomas Walsingham, became Marlowe's "patron." Thomas was also involved in spying, being responsible for espionage for Kent.

Marlowe lived in London from 1587 until his death in 1593. He ultimately lived with one Thomas Watson near Curtain Theatre on Norton Folgate. His favorable reference to the landlord had been given by the Privy Council itself.

In September 1589 while living with Watson, Marlowe was arrested and brought to trial concerning the murder of William Bradley. Bradley had engaged a thug to beat up a cousin of Watson and Watson had taken out a petition of security against him; Bradley countered his own suit but also determined to take matters into his own hand. Bradley lay in wait for Watson in an alley (Hog Lane) near his residence. Marlowe appeared and Bradley accosted him. Swords were drawn and a fight ensued, but when Watson came out, Marlowe stepped aside. The fight by sword and dagger ranged the alley, thrust and parry, and Bradley backed Watson down the alley, against a ditch (which was walled), and so desperately, Watson could not retreat further, but turned, attacked and thrust his sword into Bradley's heart. The coroner's inquiry found that death occurred "by self-defense and not by felony."

****

The "School of the Night", a political and literary camaraderie, so-called by Shakespeare, was led by Walter Raleigh, Henry Percy (Earl of Northumberland), and Henry Brooke. Percy like Raleigh would end his life in the Tower of London; he spent 16 years there. Accused of complicity in the Gunpowder Plot against James I, his only conviction occurred upon charges of tolerance for Catholics, which was true; he championed religious tolerance generally.

The group included friends of various relationships, and friends of friends, and took in scientific and charlatan pursuits, ambitions and follies. Among the members were Thomas Hariot, an astronomer, and John White, an adventurer to the Americas who brought the first Indian to England; also Dr. John Dee who was a self-professed practitioner of alchemy and the occult; his crystal ball (or "shew stone" as he called it) which was used at the pleasure of the Queen herself is now in the possession of the British Museum. Poets such as Marlowe, Edmund Spenser, Chapman (who made the acclaimed translation of Homer), Drayton, Peele, Campion were all among the circle too.

The distinguished, if controversial, luminary of the School of Night was Giordano Bruno, a one-time Dominican monk, now wandering scholar. His novel concept of a universe stretching out to infinity—literally the sky had depth where before and to men's minds still the sky was supposed to be a crystalline sphere upon which the planets and stars were illuminations spaced or moving by patterns ordained and eternal—threatened the order of mind and men. The deity God to his mind was "all-pervading" as an essence, rather than a ruler, and thus given to challenge the conceptions of the church and protestants alike. A poetic expression of such a deity is offered by Marlowe in *Tamburlaine*:

> ".... He that sits on high and never sleeps,
> Nor in one place is circumscriptible,
> But everywhere fills every continent
> With strange infusion of his sacred vigour...."

Bruno's *De Immenso et Innumerabilibus* declares

> "... every spirit and soul has a certain continuity with the spirit of the universe, so that it has its being and existence not only there where it perceives and lives, but it is also by its essence and substance diffused throughout immensity as was realized by many Platonists and Pythagoreans.... Does not this simple spirit insinuate itself into all things pervading completely and everywhere throughout the infinity of space?"

> "The one infinite is perfect, in simplicity itself, absolutely, nor can ought be greater or better. This is the one Whole, God, Universal Nature, occupying all space, of whom nought but infinity can give the perfect measure or semblance."

Wraight suggests that "...here we have the very seed of the Arian heresy which questioned the divinity of Christ on the

110

grounds that a mere man, subject to earthly passions and sufferings, however noble in himself, could not be equated with the majesty of God."

Thus, Bruno anticipated certain modern views: the philosophical bases to scientific thought, by predicate of philosophy and not experimentation or scientific knowledge; the idea of "innate necessity" is like the concept of gravity in that it caused all motion and all change; the idea that all is relative to one another by state and being and relative by point of view; the extension of atomic theory to a construct of material reality, by his vision that all matter consists of "minima" and "monads" which in turn may combine to different forms.

Bruno was executed by the Catholic authorities in 1600.

****

Another loose affiliation of like-minded persons called themselves the "University Wits" after their association with Cambridge, for which there was rivalry to that other University at Oxford. Cambridge by association was Protestant while Oxford had been and remained the "catholic" university.

Among those in the group was Robert Greene, actor and sometime playwright, who accused Marlowe publicly, and in print, of atheism, even at his death bed in 1592.

Whether jealous or by other motive, Greene reviled Marlowe from the start of his public career, calling Tamburlaine atheist and sneering at Marlowe's birth (as a cobbler's son).

****

In the spring of 1593 riots threatened London by reason of economic and social unrest due to discontent concerning alien "protestant" refugees. Plague also fitfully threatened. Almost 11,000 persons will have ultimately died of plague in that year. Marlowe himself left London to escape the plague and took up residence at Scadbury, a manor of Thomas Walsingham.

The Council of the Star Chamber issued proclamation on May 11 to arrest persons who were suspected of fomenting unrest by diatribe. One of those arrested was Thomas Kyd who had collaborated to write a play *Sir Thomas More* which by its subject would rankle the protestant authorities, but which also contained explicit references to alien refugees from another time when such caused discontent.

Under the order of the Star Council Kyd's chambers were searched and papers confiscated. Among those papers was an anonymous tract of heretical views, alleged to be "Arian" heresy, that is, a denial of Christ's divinity. In fact, the document had been originally published in 1549 as a refutation of that heresy. At any rate, under threat of torture, Kyd told the Council that the papers belonged to Marlowe and indeed, in support of Kyd, it is believed that it was this actual tract that one occasion he read to Raleigh and the School of the Night in one of their "sessions." The attention shifted from sedition to these atheist papers as there was no grounds for finding sedition, though Kyd was kept in the Tower and tortured nonetheless.

Richard Baines, a hired government informer, was set to task to prove the case against Marlowe and later would author a bill of accusations for various alleged heretical remarks by Marlowe.

On May 18th, 19th or 20th Marlowe was arrested at Scadbury and brought before the Star Chamber. There is no record of those proceedings, for all proceedings were secret. But Marlowe was immediately released on bail. Marlowe took up residence at Deptford Strand, still removed from the plague abounding London, but near enough to comply with the daily attendance required by the Star Chamber.

On or about May 27th Baines delivered to the Privy Council his indictment of Marlowe. The litany of the indictment includes that Marlowe had these contrary opinions: that Indian artifacts predate the Biblical date of creation; that Moses was a juggler and Heriots (the astronomer and friend of Raleigh) could do more than he; that Moses made the Jews to travel for 15 years a journey that should have taken them one year; that religion was only meant to keep men in awe; that Christ was a bastard and his mother dishonest; that Christ

112

was son of a carpenter and the Jews did well to crucify him; that if there is any good religion it is that of the papist because they have better ceremonies, such as elevation of the mass, shaven crowns, organs, singing men, etc.; that all protestants are hypocritical asses; that the woman of Samaria and her sister were whores and Christ knew them dishonestly; that St John the Evangelist was Christ's bedfellow; that Marlowe had as good a right to make coins as the Queen of England; that Christ would have reinstituted the holy sacrament with more ceremony than the Church of England had, and it would have included the tobacco pipe; that one Ric Cholmley swears he was converted to atheism by Marlowe.

There was no accusation of treason or sedition. It's hard to take these indictments seriously. But in at least two instances and perhaps by other inferences it seems that they are aimed indirectly at Raleigh and the School of the Night.

On May 30th Marlowe was killed at a brawl in a public house in Deptford Strand. The death is a matter of controversy, first because it followed so closely upon his arrest and Baines indictment, and second because of its unlikely description, and third by the suspicious circumstances of the men involved. But there is nothing to conclusively dispute the facts found in the coroner's inquest. Four men that day and night -- Ingram Frizer (a personal manservant to Walsingham); Robert Poley (whom Marlowe knew by their mutual involvement in espionage during the Babington Plot); Nicholas Skeres (who was friend to Poley and somehow involved with him in the affairs of the Babington Plot and otherwise was known to be a "con" man); and of course Marlowe -- all met and talked for some 10 hours in a rented room off a garden at an inn in Deptford. At six o'clock after taking supper a dispute broke out over the paying of the bill, and it is said that Marlowe made a malicious remark to Frizer and then from the bed on which he had been lying he drew the dagger from Frizer's "back" and attacked him with it, wounding his face or scalp; Frizer struggled with Marlowe and struck a mortal wound over his right eye and instantly killed him.

The coroner's inquest—which is included below—found Frizer not guilty of felonious murder.

Various theories in lieu of the coroner's findings are offered:

- That Marlowe was murdered by conspirators of the School of the Night, including Walsingham and even Raleigh, who feared that he would reveal their "atheism." But it may be that there was some other matter hidden, perhaps an intrigue with James in Scotland where it is alleged by Kyd that Marlowe intended to flee. Of course, Raleigh was enemy to James who in the end imprisoned and eventually executed him.

- That Marlowe was not murdered, but his murder feigned so he could escape. Under this theory Marlowe later wrote the Shakespearean plays and sonnets. But the plays and style of Shakespeare are more different than like Marlowe, as Rowse says; Marlowe's more intellectual and classical, and Shakespeare's more wedded to the tradition of rustic life and akin to folk tale.

A.L. Rowse, Christopher Marlowe, *His Life and Work*, Grosset & Dunlap: New York, 1964.

Excerpt(s):

The Government Agent

Lord Burghley, Queen Elizabeth's chief minister who, together with her Secretary of State, Sir Francis Walsingham, was said to rule the land with the Queen as the Head of all, was also Chancellor of the University of Cambridge. As such he used the University as his recruiting ground to enlist bright, patriotic young men to serve as secret agents. Evidently Marlowe was picked out for this service, which was vitally important in this age of Catholic versus Protestant political intrigue, an age of political assassinations, directed against the Heads of States.

In 1584, William the Silent, Prince of Orange, leader of the Protestants in the Netherlands, was assassinated following a failed attempt in 1582. In 1589, King Henry III of France, a Catholic who had flirted with Queen Elizabeth and also patronized Giordano Bruno whom the Holy Roman Inquisition burned at the stake in 1600, was assassinated with the poisoned dagger of a Jacobin friar. His brother, Charles IX, had also been poisoned. In 1610 the next King of France, Henry IV, the former champion of the Huguenots, who embraced Catholicism on ascending the throne with the words 'Paris is worth a Mass', met his death at the point of a dagger also.

The Catholic plots against Queen Elizabeth were ceaseless, but all were uncovered one after another by the English Secret Service, skillfully built up under the direction of Sir Francis Walsingham to become the greatest and most successful espionage network of the time, with agents placed as far away as Turkey to cover every exigency. It was entirely thanks to the efficiency and dedication of Walsingham's Secret Service that Queen Elizabeth led such a charmed life and escaped assassination.

Marlowe's first important assignment as a secret agent was
evidently in 1584, when he had 'proved' himself by
successfully gaining his B.A., (a hurdle many students evaded
or failed,) when his normally constant residence at his college
was suddenly interrupted by lengthy absences. We have the
invaluable records of the college buttery and audit books to
confirm this, for the weekly one shilling stipend for the
purchase of extra food and drink at the buttery bar was not
collected, and the Audit book records all presences and
absences term by term, covering also the vacations, for the
students were required to remain at college all year except for
the summer vacation.

The Babington Plot

Contemporaneous with Marlowe's absences was the plotting
of the most dangerous conspiracy yet hatched, the Babington
Plot, which was conceived at the Catholic Seminary at Rheims
run by Cardinal Allen. Students who were not Catholics were
also admitted there, probably in the hope of converting them,
and the rumor spread at Cambridge that Christopher Marlowe
had gone to Rheims as a Catholic convert. When this reached
the ears of the Cambridge authorities, they decided to
withhold permission for him to receive his M.A. degree. In
dismay it is evident that Marlowe appealed to the Privy
Council to intervene to clear his name, which they did at
once, and handsomely, in the following letter dated 29th June
1587.

'Whereas it was reported that Christopher Marlowe was
determined to have gone beyond the seas to Rheims, and
there to remain, their Lordships thought good to certify that
he had no such intent, but that in all his actions he had
behaved himself orderly and discreetly, whereby he had done
Her Majesty good service, & deserved to be rewarded for his
faithful dealing. Their Lordships' request was that the rumour
thereof should be allayed by all possible means, and that he
should be furthered in the degree he was to take this next
Commencement, because it was not Her Majesty's pleasure
that anyone employed, as he had been, in matters touching
the benefit of his country, should be defamed by those that
are ignorant in the' affairs he went about.'

The letter is signed by:

The Archbishop of Canterbury, John Whitgift.
The Lord Treasurer, Lord Burghley.
The Chancellor, Sir Christopher Hatton.
The Lord Chamberlain, Henry Carey, 1st Lord Hunsdon.
Mr. Comptroller, Sir William Knollys.

The Queen is mentioned twice, citing her personal interest in this young man's attainment of his M.A. without hindrance from the authorities who are 'ignorant of the' affairs he went about,' (quite a slap in the eye for the Cambridge top brass!) and testifies that he had done good service and 'deserved to be rewarded for his faithful dealing'. This letter is unique in the annals of Elizabethan espionage records.

Marlowe had clearly been engaged in an important assignment for the Government and had acquitted himself worthily, and all the evidence of the circumstances strongly suggests that it was in connection with the uncovering of the Babington Plot, which aimed directly at the assassination of Queen Elizabeth and her chief ministers and purposed the enthronement of Mary Queen of Scots as England's Catholic Queen. It was the most daring and dangerous plot conceived to date over which Mendoza, the Spanish Ambassador in Paris, was rubbing his hands with glee! However, Charles Nicholl, author of 'The Reckoning: The Murder of Christopher Marlowe', claims that Marlowe never went to Rheims at all. Yet since the letter states that he did not intend *there to remain* obviously he must have *been* there!

Nicholl claims that Marlowe's government employment was to do some 'snooping' on his fellow students at Cambridge to find any who were harbouring Catholic Sympathies which *might* lead them to defect to Rheims and there indulge in plotting with Elizabeth's enemies. That is what he claims constituted 'matters touching the benefit of his country' which drew from the Privy Council their letter of commendation and praise from Her Majesty! This does not make sense as 'snooping' and would not justify his well documented absence from Cambridge.

Several other scholars, less virulent than Nicholl, find it difficult to accept that Marlowe was the discreet, well-behaved, patriotic young man described in the Privy Council's letter of commendation, to whom an important task 'touching the benefit of the country' had been entrusted.

Marlowe made his mark with the Queen and her Government at the age of twenty, and he emerged as the new poet-dramatist of genius, "the Muse's Darling", at the age of twenty-three when he arrived in London. He was to continue his career in the Queen's service as a highly trusted secret agent, as we now know from further significant research published during 1996. This career brought Marlowe into close contact with the Elizabethan court and gave him also first-hand insight into the political scene in some of the major courts of Europe. This is reflected in his political play about the turmoil in France, *The Massacre at Paris*, which has regrettably survived only in a mutilated edition of what must have been a great contemporary historical drama. Even in its much-abbreviated form it is still worth performing:

Here is the speech spoken by the dying King Henry III of France after he has been stabbed by the Jacobin Friar who gained access to the king under the pretence of delivering a letter.

The English Agent, who has no words to speak, could have been Marlowe himself!

Enter the English Agent.

Henry:
Agent for England, send thy mistress word
What this detested Jacobin hath done.
Tell her, for all this, that I hope to live;
Which if I do, the papal monarch goes
To wrack, and th' antichristian kingdom falls.
These bloody hands shall tear his triple crown,
And fire accursed Rome about his ears;
I'll fire his crazed buildings, and enforce
The papal towers to kiss the lowly earth.
Navarre, give me thy hand: I here do swear
To ruinate that wicked Church of Rome,
That hatcheth up such bloody practices;
And here protest eternal love to thee,
And to the Queen of England specially,
Whom God hath bless'd for hating papistry.

Henry dies because the dagger was poisoned, but here is shown making a pact of friendship with the King of Navarre, the leader of the Huguenots who suffered dreadful slaughter in the blood-bath of St. Bartholomew's Eve in 1572, when 3,000 men, women and even babes in arms were massacred by the Catholic faction. The river Seine ran red with blood!

This massacre is the title of Marlowe's play. He was eight years old when this happened, and Canterbury received an influx of Huguenot refugees to whom Queen Elizabeth granted asylum and gave them the Undercroft of the Cathedral to use for their worship. The feelings of horror that this massacre engendered are reflected in the passion expressed by Marlowe in this speech.

The Death of Christopher Marlowe

On 30th May 1593, a murder was said to have been committed in a room that had been hired for a private meeting in a respectable house in Deptford, owned by Dame Eleanor Bull. It was not a tavern as is often alleged. Dame Bull had court connections. Her sister, Blanche, was the goddaughter of Blanche Parry, who had been the much loved nanny of the infant Elizabeth and was a "cousin" of Lord Burghley. Now widowed, Dame Bull hired out rooms and served meals. It was likely that her home was a safe house for Government Agents.

The strange circumstances of Marlowe's murder in that room at Deptford have been the subject of endless debate and conflicting theories. The following is the official story as related in the Coroner's Report, discovered by Dr. Leslie Hotson in 1925 in the archives of the Public Records Office, London.

Four men were present at Dame Bull's house on that day:

1) ROBERT POLEY, an experienced government agent, who carried the Queen's most secret and important letters in post to and from the courts of Europe. He arrived at Deptford direct from The Hague, where he had been on the Queen's business - Deptford then

being a busy naval dockyard and port from which ships voyaged back and forth to the Continent.

2)   INGRAM FRIZER, the personal servant and business agent of Marlowe's patron, the wealthy Thomas Walsingham, cousin of the recently deceased Secretary of State, Sir Francis Walsingham, who had created the espionage service which protected Queen Elizabeth's life from the on-going Catholic assassination plots. Thomas Walsingham had assisted his illustrious cousin as his right-hand man and was himself a master-spy.

3)   NICHOLAS SKERES, a minor cog in the great Walsingham spy machine, who often assisted Poley. A shady character, who was, at this time, engaged in a double-dealing project with Ingram Frizer to fleece a naive young man of his money (termed "conny-catching" by the Elizabethans). In fact, Skeres, Frizer and Poley were all skillful con-men and liars.

4)   CHRISTOPHER MARLOWE, the famous poet-dramatist, who enjoyed both the friendship and the patronage of Thomas Walsingham and at whose estate, Scadbury in Kent, he was staying at the time of his arrest, having gone there to escape the plague in London.

Thomas Walsingham therefore can be seen to be connected with all four of these men.

The day of Marlowe's arrest was Sunday, 20th May. The charge was Atheism, which was a heresy and a most serious crime, the ultimate penalty for which was burning at the stake. As it was a Sunday, the Court of Star Chamber was closed, so Marlowe was taken to the Palace of Nonsuch, where the Court was in residence.

Despite the seriousness of the charge he was not hauled off to prison to be stretched on the rack - as his fellow playwright, Thomas Kyd, had been - but was granted bail on condition that he report his presence daily to the court.

A Star Chamber informer, Richard Baines, was then set on Marlowe's track to assemble an incriminating dossier against

120

him in order to bring him to trial at the Court of Star Chamber as an Atheist. This powerful court was the judicial arm of both Church and State and was authorised to extract confession by torture, employing the same draconian methods as the Holy Roman Inquisition and operating without a jury.

Baines assembled a lethal catalogue of Marlowe's supposed blasphemous and atheistic utterances which he may well have garnered by questioning frightened people who had allegedly heard him speak them.

On Wednesday 30th May, which would have been his last day of liberty, as his bail had run out, Marlowe left Scadbury, presumably in the company of Ingram Frizer, to make his way to Deptford for a meeting with the other men described above.

"A note containing the opinion of one Christopher Marly concerning his damnable judgment of religion, and scorn of God's word:

"That the Indians, and many authors of antiquity, have assuredly written of above 16 thousand years agone, whereas Adam is proved to have lived within six thousand years.

"He affirmeth that Moses was but a juggler, and that one Hariot being Sir Walter Raleigh's man can do more than he.

"That Moses made the Jews to travel 40 years in the wilderness (which journey might have been done in less than one year) ere they came to the promised land, to the intent that those who were privy to many of his subtleties might perish, and so an everlasting superstition reign in the hearts of the people.

"That the beginning of religion was only to keep men in awe.

"That it was an easy matter for Moses being brought up in all the arts of the Egyptians to abuse the Jews, being a rude and gross people.

"That Christ was a bastard and his mother dishonest.

"That he was the son of a carpenter, and that if the Jews among whom he was born did crucify him, they best knew him and whence he came.

"That Christ deserved better to die than Barabas, and that the Jews made a good choice, though Barabas were both a thief and a murderer.

"That if there be any God or any good religion, then it is in the Papists, because the service of God is performed with more ceremonies, as elevation of the mass, organs, singing men, shaven crowns, etc. That all Protestants are hypocritical asses.

"That if he were put to write a new religion, he would undertake both a more excellent and admirable method, and that all the New Testament is filthily written.

"That the woman of Samaria and her sister were whores and that Christ knew them dishonestly.

"That Saint John the Evangelist was bedfellow to Christ and leaned always in his bosom; that he used him as the sinners of Sodoma

'That all they that love not tobacco and boys are fools.

"That all the apostles were fishermen and base fellows, neither of wit nor worth; that Paul only had wit, but he was a timorous fellow in bidding men to be subject to magistrates against his conscience.

"That he had as good a right to coin as the Queen of England, and that he was acquainted with one Poole, a prisoner in Newgate, who hath great skill in mixture of metals, and having learned some things of him, he meant through help of a cunning stamp-maker to coin French crowns, pistolets, and English shillings.

"That if Christ would have instituted the sacrament with more ceremonial reverence, it would have been in more admiration; that it would have been better much better being administered in a tobacco pipe.

"That the angel Gabriel was bawd to the Holy Ghost, because he brought the salutation to Mary.

"That one Richard Cholmley hath confessed that he was persuaded by Marlowe's reasons to become an atheist."

Source Document: Coroner's Report translated from the
Latin by Leslie Hotson for his book *The Death of Christopher
Marlowe*

.... About the tenth hour before noon (the
afore said gentlemen) met together in a room in the
house of a certain Eleanor Bull, widow; & there
passed the time together & dined & after dinner
were in quiet sort together & walked in the garden
belonging to the said house until the sixth hour after
noon of the same day & then returned from the said
garden to the room aforesaid & there together and
in company supped; & after supper the said Ingram
& Christopher Morley were in speech & uttered one
to the other divers malicious words for the reason
that they could not be at one nor agree about the
payment of the sum of pence, that is le recknynge,
there; & the said Christopher Morley then lying
upon a bed in the room where they supped, &
moved with anger against the said Ingram ffrysar
upon the words aforesaid spoken between them,
and the said Ingram then & there sitting in the room
aforesaid with his back towards the bed where the
said Christopher Morley was then lying, sitting near
the bed, that is, nere the bed, & with the front part
of his body towards the table & the aforesaid
Nicholas Skeres & Robert Poley sitting on either
side of the said Ingram in such a manner that the
same Ingram ffrysar in no wise could take flight; it
so befell that the said Christopher Morley on a
sudden & of his malice towards the said Ingram
aforethought, then & there maliciously drew the
dagger of the said Ingram which was at his back, and
with the same dagger the said Christopher Morley
then & there maliciously gave the aforesaid Ingram
two wounds on his head of the length of two inches
& of the depth of a quarter of an inch; where-upon
the said Ingram, in fear of being slain, & sitting in
the manner aforesaid between the said Nicholas
Skeres & Robert Poley so that he could not in any
wise get away, in his own defence & for the saving
of his life, then & there struggled with the said
Christopher Morley to get back from him his dagger
aforesaid; in which affray the same Ingram could not

get away from the said Christopher Morley; & so it befell in that affray that the said Ingram, in defence of his life, with the dagger aforesaid to the value of 12d, gave the said Christopher then & there a mortal wound over his right eye of the depth of two inches & of the width of one inch; of which mortal wound the aforesaid Christopher Morley then & there instantly died; & so the Jurors aforesaid say upon their oath that the said Ingram killed & slew Christopher Morley aforesaid on the thirtieth day of May in the thirtyfifth year named above at Detford Strand aforesaid within the verge in the room aforesaid within the verge in the manner and form aforesaid in the defence and saving of his own life, against the peace of our said lady the Queen, her now crown & dignity; & further the said Jurors say upon their oath that the said Ingram after the slaying aforesaid perpetrated & done by him in the manner & form aforesaid neither fled nor withdrew himself; But what goods or chattels, lands or tenements the said Ingram had at the time of the slaying aforesaid, done and perpetrated by him in the manner & form aforesaid, the said Jurors are totally ignorant. In witness of which thing the said Coroner as well as the Jurors aforesaid to this Inquisition have interchangeably set their seals.

Given the day & year above named &c. 'by WILLIAM DANBY Coroner'.

Background—Legend of Faust or Faustus

Paul A. Bates, *Faust: Sources, Works, Criticism*, Harcourt, Brace & World Inc.: New York, 1969.

Faustus was first staged in 1594, a year after Marlowe's death. It was first published in 1604 and then again in 1616; the first version called the A version and the second called the B; the second is longer and contains elements that some dispute to be authentic, among which is the element of a parallel farce.

The original reference, which Marlowe must have employed, as his play tracks it so well, is the so-called *Faustbuch*, published in 1587, which in turn is based upon the life of one who lived in Germany and for whom there are a number of contemporaneous records. See: Johann Speis of Frankfurt, *Historia von D. Johann Fausten*, 1587.

John Faustus who self-bestowed his doctoral title, lived in the late 15th century until about 1540. The earliest record of him is 1507. He was a magician or conjurer who traveled Germany, more or less welcome, making his livelihood by his demonstrations and practice of magic. His sobriquet, Faustus, was borrowed from the allusion to Simon Magus, who was called "faustus" (Latin for "the chosen one"). Marlowe was not the first to exploit the legend of Faustus for dramatic effect. The story had become a cautionary, or morality tale, employed by protestant leaders who were worried about the spread of religious skepticism: here was a tale of damnation specific to the "aspiring mind." Among those religious leaders interested in this legend was Luther himself.

The editor suggests in his introduction that with the development of scientific rationalism by Bacon and Descartes the attitude toward Faust changed. Future writers would "save" Faust, starting with Lessing in a play of 1759 that does not survive, and most notably then by Goethe.

The reference for this history is *The Sources of the Faust Tradition from Simon Magus to Lessing*, Philip Mason Palmer and Robert Pattison More, Oxford University Press: New York, 1966.

According to various historical sources letters and journals and other private and public records -- the original person was named George Sabellicus, later called George Faust, later Doctor Johann Faustus. [See below in the edited version of the Book an editor's analysis of this confused history]. He was a sometime school teacher, sometime vagabond, who claimed to be a "necromancer." Called by others a braggart, he was banned from some towns and punished in others, in others still he was wittingly employed to give his magical or prophetical services. He called himself "philosopher of philosophers." A sermon by protestant clergyman of Basle (Johannes Gast) contains tales of Faust's magic, including the belief that he was accompanied by a dog and horse that were demons and that the dog would assume the shape of his servant to serve the evening meal. Another contemporary recites the legend of the flight and fall of Faustus (which event was actually borrowed from the legend of Simon Magus).

The History of Doctor Johann Faustus, trans. H.G. Halle, University of Illinois Press: Urbana, 1965.

This is an edited version of the manuscript of the German Faustbuch, dated mid 1580's. It removes copyists gloss and errors and additions in so far as it can. The original "novel" was written by an unknown author about 1580. This manuscript survives in the Duke-August library of Wolfenbuttel. Leibinz and Lessing, who retold versions of the legend, had been librarians there.

The editor Halle reviews the history of the Faust legend with these observations and conclusions:

- The original Faust, if there was one, was a person named Georg Faust (Faust being a common German surname) who appeared in historical record in 1520 in a ledger entry of the Bishop of Bamberg in receipt of a payment of 10 Gulden for the Bishop's astrological chart.

- Other, more vague references include a letter warning a friend of a braggart and fool named Faustus (1513), and reference in another letter (1507) about a practitioner of Black Magic named George Sabellicus who called himself "Faustus junior." This last reference reminds us that (1) there were many who practiced magic arts in those days and made their living thereby, and that there was popular association of magic to the figure of Faustus (Simon Magus) and perhaps it was a "stage name." [This editor does not make that connection but thinks there may have been another magician.]

- Other letters and public records reference Georg Faust or Faustus as an astrologist, a necromancer, a magician throughout a period of 1520 to 1540 when his violent death is reported as murder at the hands of the Devil.

- He is called variously a philosopher, demigod, "Devil's Brother-in-Law"; Martin Luther references him in his *Table Talk*, as does Luther's disciple, Philip Melanchthon; two cities bar his entry by proclamation (Nuremberg in 1532 and Ingolstadt in 1528)

- The editor suggests that the subsequent association of the legend to Johann Faust was an error by Melanchthon who mistook the original for another person he had known while attending the University of Heidelberg

- At any rate, after the supposed death of Georg Faust in 1540, references to Johann Faust increased but now these references seemed fed by folklore rather than historic incident.

A first collection of Faust tales was made by Wolf Wambach, a town chronicler for Erfurt; it does not survive.

The editor says this of this first version

"... Faust first takes on the characteristic personality which made him so attractive to poets of subsequent ages. It is the character of a brilliant heretic among stuffy academicians, of a researcher into forbidden knowledge feared by the professors. Wambach's Faust, when lecturing on Homer at the University of Erfurt, conjures up some heroes and other figures form the Trojan War. Their aspects so frightening—Cyclops appears with Greeks dangling from his teeth—that the audience runs away. When some professors express mild regrets that so many classics have been lost, Faust volunteers to recover all the works of Plautus and Terence; but the professors of theology will not allow it, insisting that the Devil could well slip in all sorts of objectionable and improper passages....
In a last tale, a Franciscan Monk tries to convert Faust and promises to say many masses on his behalf. 'Here a mass, there a mass,' growls Faust, 'my pledge binds me too hard.' He had given the Devil his word and is too proud to go back on it." (Pg. 6)

The second collection of Faust tales is from Christoph Rosshirt of Nuremberg in the 1570's. This version embraces another tradition of the Faust legend. Faust employs the black arts for the good life. A series of stories that the author suggests originate from independent folklore, motifs and vignettes that have another life, apart from the Faust legend. Some of these are stories of other magicians. Some are stories having nothing to do with magicians per se but contain element of sorcery or magic.

So, for example:

- He serves guests food and drink stolen from the court of the King of England and transports the crowd of them in an instant to English court;

- He borrows money from a Jew and refuses to pay him back; when the Jew comes to get the money, he pretends to sleep; pulling on his leg to awaken him, Faust's leg is pulled off and the Jew flees, fearing he will be accused of murder

- Faust charms some bundles of straw to appear as fat swine; he warns the buyer to avoid the river, but when the buyer drives them into the water, they disintegrate and float away

> "Rosshirt's stories are not new ones at all, but merely rehashing of ancient tricks which magicians and other rascals had been playing on the people for centuries. Now all these tales begin to be connected with Faust, so that his figure becomes a collage of many personalities, some historical and some of them legendary."

The German *Faustbuch* is the third collection of tales, emerging in 1580. The author points out the specifically Protestant themes of the book: it is anyway specifically anti-Catholic. But the central issue of Grace and Salvation, and the deserts of the well-intentioned man underlies it but ironically, since Faust is only a cynical penitent if penitent at all. This version is the one translated in this book, but it too was corrupted by copyist over even the brief interval of its manuscript to its publication in the new media of typeset printing.

The printed version was made by Johann Spies of Frankfurt in 1587, using one of the corrupted manuscripts of the unknown author of the original *Faustbuch*. "A couple of the more salacious chapters and some of the more insolent remarks were deleted, many a pious moral was drawn, and numerous Christian admonitions were added and Speis had produced the money-maker of the century. Although he did not get the book off his presses until the fall of 1587, two more printings were required before the year was out, in which eight new Faust tales had been added."

Over the next decade it was rapidly translated into many European tongues, including English. The English version appears in print before 1592 although that is the imprimatur of the earliest surviving edition.

The editor cites these general social conditions of the day:

(1)   "a religious revival" in both protestant and catholic society, stimulating each one the other by the affront each one was to the other;

(2)   the printing press, making circulation of ideas easier, wider, faster; and I should say a liberty to thinking;

(3)   the rise of merchant classes and "democratic" cities in which the merchants rather than the nobility determined political and legal matters;

(4)   alienation of and reaction by nobility that is displaced by the merchant classes (the original *bourgeoisie*); a reaction that was sometimes brutal, sometimes calculated; in the early 16th century some nobility reverted to ancient form, challenging commerce and traffic, as would a pirate, commanding rivers from castles and confiscating goods at will, by right and by arms;

(5)   the Peasant Revolution - see the autobiography of *Gotz von Berlichgen With the Iron Hand*; or life of Franz von Sickingen (said to be a friend of Faustus); or the life of Ulrich von Hutten who although a knight sympathized with the Revolt, was a Protestant, and a highly literate Humanist (died of syphilis); Hutten's cousin references Faustus in a letter from Venezuela in which he recalls that Faustus had predicted catastrophe, for all were dying of syphilis.

Sources of Legend:
Faust Chapbook of 1587.

> Source: Abstracted from Historia von D. Johann
> Fausten (Frankfurt am Main: Johann Spies, 1587).

Johann Faustus was born in Roda in the province of Weimar, of God-fearing parents.

Although he often lacked common sense and understanding, at an early age he proved himself a scholar, mastering not only the Holy Scriptures, but also the sciences of medicine, mathematics, astrology, sorcery, prophesy, and necromancy.

These pursuits aroused in him a desire to commune with the Devil, so--having made the necessary evil preparations--he repaired one night to a crossroads in the Spesser Forest near Wittenberg. Between nine and ten o'clock he described certain circles with his staff and thus conjured up the Devil.

Feigning anger at having been summoned against his will, the Devil arrived in the midst of a great storm. After the winds and lightning had subsided the Devil asked Dr. Faustus to reveal his will, to which the scholar replied that he was willing to enter into a pact. The Devil, for his part, would agree: 1. to serve Dr. Faustus for as long as he should live, and 2. to provide Dr. Faustus with whatever information he might request, and 3. never to utter an untruth to Dr. Faustus.

The Devil agreed to these particulars, on the condition that Dr. Faustus would promise: 1. at the expiration of twenty-four years to surrender his body and soul to the Devil, 2. to confirm the pact with a signature written in his own blood, and 3. to renounce his Christian faith.

Having reached an agreement, the pact was drawn up, and Dr. Faustus formalized it with his own blood.

Henceforth Dr. Faustus' life was filled with comfort and luxury but marked by excess and perversion. Everything was within his grasp: elegant clothing, fine wines, sumptuous food, beautiful women--even Helen of Troy and the concubines from the Turkish sultan's harem. He became the most famous astrologer in the land, for his horoscopes never failed. No

longer limited by earthly constraints, he traveled from the
depths of hell to the most distant stars. He amazed his
students and fellow scholars with his knowledge of heaven
and earth.

However, for all his fame and fortune, Dr. Faustus could not
revoke the twenty-four-year limit to the Devil's indenture.
Finally recognizing the folly of his ways, he grew ever more
melancholy. He bequeathed his worldly goods to his young
apprentice, a student named Christoph Wagner from the
University of Wittenberg .

Shortly after midnight on the last day of the twenty-fourth
year, the students who had assembled at the home of the
ailing Dr. Faustus heard a great commotion. First came the
sound of a ferocious storm and then the shouts--first
terrifyingly loud then ever weaker--from their mentor.

At daybreak they ventured into his room. Bloodstains were
everywhere. Bits of brain clung to the walls. Here they
discovered an eye, and there a few teeth. Outside they found
the corpse, its members still twitching, lying on a manure pile.

His horrible death thus taught them the lesson that had
escaped their master during his lifetime: to hold fast to the
ways of God, and to reject the Devil and all his temptations.

Sources of Legend:
Dr. Faust at Boxberg Castle, Germany

Source: August Schnezler, Badisches Sagen-Buch
(Karlsruhe: Verlag von W. Creuzbauer, 1846), v. 2,
pp. 613-614. * Schnezler's source: Oral tradition, as
recorded by Bernhard Baader in Mone's Anzeiger
fŸr Kunde teutscher Vorzeit, 1838. This legend was
also published in Bernard Baader, Volksagen aus dem
Lande Baden und den angrenzenden Gegenden
(Karlsruhe: Verlag der Herder'schen Buchhandlung,
1851), no. 367, pp. 327-328. The story of hypnotic
deception in the garden is reminiscent of an episode
at the end of the Auerbach's Cellar scene in Goethe's
Faust, part one.

When Dr. Faust was in Heilbronn, performing his
troublesome arts throughout the region, he often went to
Boxberg Castle, where he was always courteously received.

Once he was there on a cold winter's day, strolling with the
lords and ladies of the palace along the garden paths on the
east side of the castle. The ladies complained about the frost,
and he immediately caused the sun to shine warmly, the snow-
covered ground to turn green, and a mass of violets and
beautiful flowers of every kind to spring forth. Then at his
command the trees blossomed, and -- following the desires of
the group -- apples, plums, peaches, and other good fruit
ripened on the branches. Finally, he caused grape vines to
grow and bear grapes. He then invited each of his companions
to cut off a grape, but not before he gave the signal to do so.
When all of them were ready to cut away he removed the
deception from their eyes, and each one saw that he was
holding a knife against the nose of the person next to him.
The part of the garden where this took place has ever since
been called "the violet garden."

Another time Faust left Boxberg Castle at a quarter past
eleven in order to be at a banquet in Heilbronn at the last
strike of twelve o'clock. He got into his carriage hitched to
four black horses and drove away like the wind, and he did
indeed arrive in Heilbronn punctually at the strike of twelve.

A man working in a field saw how horned spirits paved the way before the carriage, while others pulled up the paving stones from behind and carried them away, thus destroying every trace of the pavement.

Sources of Legend:
Dr. Faust's Hell-Master, Germany

Source: Joh. Aug. Ernst Kšhler, Sagenbuch des Erzgebirges (Schneeberg and Schwarzenberg: Verlag und Druck von Carl Moritz GŠrtner, 1886), no. 277, p. 229.

According to legend, there is a book, named Dr. Faust's Hell-Master, which teaches the art of controlling spirits, even of making the devil subservient to oneself. It is said to be buried beneath a thorn bush behind the Chemnitz Castle, on the road to the Kuch Forest. Many advocates of the black art have unsuccessfully attempted to find this book.

Sources of Legend:
Dr. Faust in Erfurt, Germany

> Source: J. G. Th. Grässe, Sagenbuch des Preußischen Staats, vol. 1 (Glogau: Verlag von Carl Flemming, 1868), no. 453, pp. 339-340. The episode with the drunken companions was incorporated into the Auerbach's Cellar scene of Goethe's Faust, part one.

At one time the renowned Dr. Faust sojourned in Erfurt. He lived in Michelsgasse next to the great Collegium.

As a learned professor and with the permission of the academic senate he lectured in the large auditorium of the Collegium Building about Greek poets. Indeed, he explained Homer to his audience, the students, describing the heroic figures of the Iliad and the Odyssey so realistically that the students expressed their desire to see them with their own eyes. He made this possible, conjuring them up from the underworld, but when the students saw the powerful giant Polyphemus, they all became terrified and wanted to see or hear nothing more from him.

He drove through the narrowest street in Erfurt with a double-span load of hay, for which reason this street has ever since been called "Dr. Faust's Street."

Once he came riding a horse that ate and ate and could never be satisfied.

Another time he tapped all kinds of wine from a wooden table and made the drunken drinking companions think that they saw grapes. They wanted to cut them from the vines, but when he caused the deceptive image to disappear, each one had another one's nose in his fingers instead of wine grapes.

A house in Schössergasse is said to still have an opening in the roof that can never be closed with roofing tiles because Faust used it for his cloak rides.

He is said to have created a magnificent winter garden and provided delicious meals for numerous noble guests, thus achieving a high reputation.

Soon everyone in Erfurt was talking of nothing but Dr. Faust, and it was feared that a great many people would be led astray through his devilish arts.

Thus, a learned monk by the name of Dr. Klinge was sent to convert him. But Faust did not want to be converted. In response to the masses and prayers directed at tearing him away from the devil, Dr. Faust said, "No, my good Dr. Klinge, it would be disreputable for me to break the contract that I signed with my blood. That would be dishonest. The devil has honestly upheld his promises, and I will also keep my word with him."

"Then go to the devil, you cursed piece of devil's meat and member of the devil's band!" cried the monk angrily. "Go to the eternal fires that have been prepared for the devil and his angels!" And the monk ran to Rector Magnificus and reported to him that Dr. Faustus was a totally unrepentant sinner.

Then Faust was banished from the city of Erfurt, and never again has a sorcerer been accepted there.

Source: J. G. Th. Gršsse, Sagenbuch des Preußischen Staats, vol. 1 (Glogau: Verlag von Carl Flemming, 1868), no. 453, pp. 391-392.

Philipp Melanchton (1497-1560), humanist, classical scholar, theologian, and professor at the University of Wittenberg, was an important associate of Martin Luther in the protestant reformation.

It is not true, as some claimed as early as the middle of the sixteenth century, that Dr. Faust grew up in Wittenberg and earned a doctorate of theology there, that he lived near the outer gate and had a house and garden in a street named Schneegasse (which never existed), and that he was strangled by the devil in the village of Kimlich, a half mile from Wittenberg, in the presence of several scholars and students. However, he did spend time in Wittenberg and was tolerated there for a while, until he became so crude that they tried to imprison him, and then fled to another place.

While in Wittenberg he approached Philipp Melanchton, who read the book to him, scolding him and warning him that if he did not immediately desist from his evil ways he would come to an evil end, which did indeed happen. He did not repent.

Now one day at ten o'clock in the morning Master Philipp was leaving his study on his way downstairs to eat when Faust, who was with him at that time, and whom he had vigorously scolded, said to him: "Master Philipp, you always approach me with rough words. Someday, when you are about to sit down to a meal, I am going to cause all the pots in the kitchen to fly up the chimney, so that you and your guests will have nothing to eat."

Thereupon Philipp answered him: "Desist from such talk! I -- -- on your art!" And he did desist.

Another old God-fearing man also tried to convert him. To show his thanks, Faust sent a devil to the man's bedroom to frighten him as he was going to bed. The devil walked about in the room, grunting like a sow. The man, however, was not afraid. Armed with his faith, he ridiculed the devil: "What a fine voice you have! You are singing like an angel who was not allowed to remain in heaven because he wanted to be God's equal and was thus thrust out for his pride and now wanders through people's houses in the form of a sow!" With that the spirit, not wanting to be in a place where he was ridiculed because of his apostasy and his wickedness, returned to Faust and complained to him how he had been received there.

Dr. Faust, however, did lead a student astray. Dr. Lercheimer himself knew one of his friends well into an advanced age. This man had a crooked mouth. Whenever he wanted a hare, he would go out into the woods, make his hocus-pocus, and a hare would run right into his hands.

> Source: Ludwig Bechstein, Deutsches Sagenbuch
> (Meersburg and Leipzig: F. W. Hendel Verlag, 1930),
> no. 412, p. 285. First published 1852.

One winter the renowned Doctor Faustus came to the Count of Anhalt. Seeing that the count's wife was pregnant, Doctor Faustus asked her if she did not desire something special to eat, as is often the case with expectant mothers. He said that with the help of his magic powers he could get her anything she wanted. The countess graciously accepted his friendly offer and told him that a great desire of hers would be satisfied if she could have some fresh fruit such as grapes, cherries, and peaches, instead of the dried confection and nuts that she currently had. But she thought that neither he nor any other magician could get such things in the middle of a harsh winter.

Doctor Faustus took three silver platters, set them in front of the dining room window, muttered a magic formula, then soon returned with fresh fruit. The first platter was filled with apples, pears, and peaches; the second with cherries, apricots, and plums; and the third filled with red and green grapes. He invited the countess to partake of the fruit, which she did with great pleasure.

When it came time for Doctor Faustus to take leave of Anhalt, he requested the count and the countess to accompany him on a walk, for he wanted to show them something new. This they did, accompanied by the count's entourage. Approaching the castle gate, they saw a newly constructed palace on the hill called RombŸhl. Water birds were swimming in its broad moats. The palace had five towers. As the party came closer, they found that two of the towers and the outer yard were alive with a menagerie of rare animals which were walking a jumping about inside, without injuring one another. There were apes, monkeys, bears, chamois, ostriches, as well as other animals.

An elaborate breakfast awaited them in one of the halls. Doctor Faust's familiar, Christoph Wagner, served as waiter, and music was sounding from an unseen source. The food and wine were such that everyone ate and drank with great pleasure until they were full.

After spending more than an hour in this place, the party left the beautiful palace. As they were approaching Anhalt Castle they looked back at the new palace and saw and heard it go up in flames, with the sound of rifles and canons. Faustus and Wagner had disappeared, and they all were suddenly as hungry as lions. They had to have breakfast once again, for everything that they had eaten had been merely an illusion.

Sources of Legend:
Dr. Faustus Was a Good Man, England

Source: Henry Bett, Nursery Rhymes and Tales: Their Origin and History, 2nd edition (London: Methuen and Company, 1924), p. 72.

Dr. Faustus was a good man,
He whipped his scholars now and then,
When he whipped them he made them dance,
Out of Scotland into France,
Out of France into Spain,
And then he whipped them back again!

Sources of Legend:
Dafydd Hiraddug and the Crow Barn, Wales

Source: Elias Owen, Welsh Folk-Lore: A Collection of the Folk-Tales and Legends of North Wales, Being the Prize Essay of the National Eisteddfod, 1887 (Facsimile reprint, Felinfach: Llanerch Publishers, 1996), pp. 159-160.

There is an incredible tradition connected with this place, *Ffinant, Trefeglwys*. It is said that an old barn stands on the right-hand side of the highway.

One Sunday morning, as the master was starting to church, he told one of the servants to keep the crows from a field that had been sown with wheat, in which field the old barn stood. The servant, through some means, collected all the crows into the barn, and shut the door on them. He then followed his master to the church, who, when he saw the servant there, began to reprove him sharply. But the master, when he heard the strange news, turned his steps homewards, and found to his amazement that the tale was true, and it is said that the barn was filled with crows. This barn ever afterwards was called Crow-Barn, a name it still retains.

It is said that the servant's name was *Dafydd Hiraddug*, and that he had sold himself to the devil, and that consequently, he was able to perform feats, which in this age are considered incredible.

However, it is said that *Dafydd* was on this occasion more subtle than the old serpent, even according to the agreement which was between them. The contract was, that the devil was to have complete possession of *Dafydd* if his corpse were taken over the side of the bed, or through a door, or if buried in a churchyard, or inside a church. *Dafydd* had commanded, that on his death, the liver and lights were to be taken out of his body and thrown on the dunghill, and notice was to be taken whether a raven or a dove got possession of them; if a raven, then his body was to be taken away by the foot, and not by the side of the bed, and through the wall, and not through the door, and he was to be buried, not in the churchyard nor in the church but under the church walls. And

145

the devil, when he saw that by these arrangements he had been duped, he cried, saying:

> *Dafydd Hiraddug*, badly bred,
> False when living, and false when dead.

Excerpts of the German Faustbuch of 1587

Source: *The History of the Damnable Life and Deserved Death of Doctor John Faustus*, Speis (trans. William Rose), Dutton: New York, 1925.

From that translation: the story of how he perverted his doctor of divinity by his curiosity for other knowledge ("fell into fantasies and deep cogitations") and pursued the "Devilish Arts, and that had the Chaldean, Persian, Hebrew, Arabian, and Greek tongues, using Figures, Characters, Conjurations, Incantations, with many other ceremonies belonging to these infernal Arts as Necromancy, Charms, Soothsaying, Witchcraft, Enchantment, being delighted with their books, words and names so well that he studied day and night…"

> *"It is written no man can serve two masters: and, thou shalt not tempt the Lord thy God: but Faustus threw all this in the wind, and made his soul of no estimation, regarding more his worldly pleasure than the joys to come, therefore at the day of judgment there is no hope of his redemption."*

Faustus conjures the devil and makes a pact with him: that the devil should serve him, bring him anything that he desired and that the devil "should tell him nothing but that which is true." But Faust originally would not bargain to lose his soul and so the devil departed at his invective.

Thrice the devil and Faustus met and, in the end, would strike a bargain. It is set to writing and in his own words, Faustus says:

> *"…sithence I began to study and speculate the course and order of the Elements, I have not found through the gift that is given me from above, any such learning and wisdom, that can bring me to my desires: and for that I find, that men are unable to instruct me any farther in the matter, Now have I Doctor John Faustus, unto the hellish prince of the Orient and his messenger Mephistopheles, given*

*both body and soul, upon such condition, that they
shall learn me and fulfill my desire in all
things..."*

Hence it was for knowledge that he gave up his soul and his
salvation, that is, for liberty of mind (and liberty of
experience). The remainder of the tale by Speis takes the
form of disputations between the "spirit" and Faustus,
especially regarding the nature of Hell, and ultimately a visit to
hell, then a flight to the heavens to review the whole of the
world, and then a tour of European crown heads where
Faustus performs magic and mischief. The tale begins its
culmination with the conjuration of Helen to be his concubine
and a few more tricks, followed by torment of doubt, his will
and his death and damnation. The last of the *Faustbuch* is his
final lecture to his students: "...I beseech you let this my
lamentable end to the residue of your lives be a sufficient
warning, that you have God always before your eyes, praying
unto him that he would ever defend you from the temptation
of the Devil...."

Regarding Marlowe's Faustus, the editor comments that
Marlowe changes the temper of the legend he had received
from the *Faustbuch*: "Faustus is damned for his worldly
aspirations, yet the poetry reveals a sensuous delight in
worldly things.... Faustus is now a tragic hero, torn between
unbounded aspiration and the limitations of human life."

Summary and Excerpts:

I: *Of His Parentage And Youth:* He was sent to Wittemberg to
study theology. "Faustus strayed from this godly purpose..."
"Therefore we shall blame neither his parents nor his
patrons...." The blames rather his "cleverness" and tells us
that his companions called him the "speculator." He lived
"crassly and godlessly in gluttony and lust." He found his
"ilk" who dealt in Chaldean, Persian, Arabian and Greek
words; books, words and names for conjuring and sorcery.
He also learned the Holy Scriptures, but "All this he threw in
the wind and put his soul away for a time above the door sill,
wherefore there shall for him be no pardon."

148

II: *How Faust Did Achieve and Acquire Sorcery*: "Doctor Faustus' complexion was such that he loved what ought not be loved, and to the which his spirit did devote itself day and night, taking on eagle's winds and seekign out the very foundations of Heaven and Earth." He wanted the Devil to appear to him. His spell in the forest caused a tumultuous storm. Dancing devils, etc. A second effort on another night resulted in amazing pyrotechniques: a glowing orb of fire in midair and from it emerged a burning man and from it resolved a gray friar who greeted him. Faustus commanded him to then appear in his house the next morning.

III: *Here Followeth The Disputatio Held By Faustus And The Spirit*: At home now the spirit did appear as he was commanded. Faustus "laid before the spirit these several articles," namely, that the spirit be subservient and obedient to him, that the spirit would not withhold any information concerning his studies, that the spirit would not respond untruthfully. The spirit rejected these articles, saying that he was not his own master and would require consent of the "Oriental Prince," of Lucifer. Faustus is not prepared to accept Lucifer or his own damnation, but bids the spirit to come again.

IV: *The Second Disputatio With The Spirit*. At Vespers the spirit returns and offers obedience to Faustus in exchange for certain conditions: that Fautus should agree to a term of life; that at the end of his life, Faustus should become his "property;" that Faustus should provide a writ to this effect, "authenticated in his own blood;" that Faustus should "renounce the Christian Fatih and defy all believers." "Puffed up with pride and arrogance" Faustus accepts these terms. The spirit promises him "every lust of his heart" to be fulfilled.

V: *Doctor Faustus's Third Collogquium With The Spirit, Which Was Called Mephistophiles ●Concering Also The Pact Which These Two Made*. Faustus commanded the spirit to appear to him in the guise of a Franciscan Monk, ringing a bell as he arrived. He learned the spirits name. He exceuted a "written instrument." Faustus employed his penknife to prick a vein in his left hand so with to write. Upon this hand appeared the bloody words: "O homo fuge — id est: O mortal fly from him and do what is right."

"I, JOHANN FAUSTUS, Dr.,

Do publicly declare with mine own hand in
covenant & by power of these presents:

Whereas, mine own spiritual faculties having been
exhaustively explored (including the gifts dispensed
from above and graciously imparted to me), I still
cannot comprehend;

And whereas, it being my wish to probe further into
the matter, I do propose to speculate upon the
Elementa;

And whereas mankind doth not teach such things;

Now therefore have I summoned the spirit who
calleth himself Mephistophiles, a servant of the
Hellish Prince in Orient, charged with informing
and instructing me, and agreeing against a
promissory instrument hereby transferred unto him
to be subservient and obedient to me in all things.

I do promise him in return that, when I be fully
sated of that which I desire of him, twenty-four
years also being past, ended and expired, he may at
such a time and in whatever manner or wise pleaseth
him order, ordain, reign, rule and possess all that
may be mine: body, property, flesh, blood, etc.,
herewith duly bound over in eternity and
surrendered by covenant in mine own hand by
authority and power of these presents, as well as of
my mind, brain, intent, blood and will.

I do now defy all living beings, all the Heavenly
Host and all mankind, and this must be.

In confirmation and contract whereof I have drawn
out mine own blood for certification in lieu of a seal.

Doctor Faustus, the Adept

in the *Elementa* and in Church Doctrine"

VII: *Concerning the Service that Mephistophiles Used Toward Faustus*: A yoiung schoolboy, named for posterity as Christoph Wagner, was Faustus "famulus," whom he had promised to make a learned and worthy man. Wagner and Mephistophiles lived with him. Faustus had a "superfluity of victuals and provisions, for when he desired a good wine the spirit brought it to him from whatever cellar he liked…" He brought him cooked meat, fabrics for his apparel. "In sum, it was all stolen, wickedly borrowed goods, so that Doctor Faustus' meat and clothing was very respectable, but godless."

VIII: *Concerning Doctor Faustus' Intended Marriage*: "…Faustus' *aphrodisia* did day and night so prick him that he desired to enter matrimony and take a wife. He questioned his spirit in this regard, who was to be sure an enemy of the matrimonial estate as created and ordained by God." Mephistophiles said he would not aid this; for man cannot serve two masters, god and us devils too. "Shouldst thou promise to wed, thou shalt then most assuredly be torn into little pieces by us." When Faustus defied him, a storm blew. He fled downstairs but fire leapt up about him. The Devil himself appeared and Faustus quailed before him and agreed to give up his desire for marriage, but Mephistopheles promised that "…if thou canst not live chastely, then will I lead to thy bed any day or night whatever woman thou seest in this city or elsewhere. Whoever might please thy lust….:"

IX: *Doctor Faustus' Question of his Spirit Mephistophiles.* Faustus asks him what manner of spirit he is. To which he gives a history of the Banished Angel. It occurred after the Fall of man and Lucifer became the "enemy of God" and "did presume to work all manner of tyranny upon men—as is every day manifest when one falleth to his death; another hangeth, drowneth or stabbeth himself; a third is stabbed, driven mad, and the life…." "Because the first man was created so perfect by God, the Devil did begrudge him such." "Without number are our spirits that do insinuate themselves among men and cause them to fall."

> Note: *Mephistophiles* is a **named** demon like Beelzebub, or Asmodeus, or Belial, or Dogon. Particulars of evil about whom certain stories may be told. The names of these others originated probably from names of gods of other peoples (e.g., Belial =

Ba'al?). But *Mephistophiles* name is a literary invention. It is a Greek-sounding name, but it has no known etymology.

"So hast thou possessed me also? Sweet fellow tell me the truth. The spirit answered: Well why not? As soon as we looked upon they heart and saw with what manner of thoughts thou didst consort, how thou couldst netiher use nor get another than the Devil for such an intent and purpose, lo, we then made those thoughts and strivings yet more impioius and old, and so prurient that thou hadst no rest by day nor by night,all thine aspirations and endeavors being directed toward the accompllishment of sorcery. And even while thou didst conjure us, we were amiaking thee so wicked and so audacious that thou hadst let the very Devil fetch thee before thou hadst forsaken thy purpose…. All this, Lord Fauste, canst thou learn from thyself. It is true, quoth Doctor Faustus, there is no turning from my way now."

X: *A Disputatio Concernign the Prior State of the Banished Angels*: He asks about the fall of Lucifer. Mephistophiles replies that he had been exalted among all — " he outshone all other creatures and was an ornament beyond all other works of God, gold and precious stones, even the sun and stars." But his pride, insolence and vanity drove him to defy God who then cast him to hell where he must stay forever. Faust went to his bedchamber and laid on his bed and wept bitterly: "O woe is me and ever woe! Even so will it come to pass with me also…" But he was not penitent and did not offer resistance to the Devil. The author tells us: "Even if he had been compelled to yield up his body here, his soul would nevertheless have been saved."

XI: *A Disputatio Concerning Hell, How It Was Created and Fashioned; Concerning Also the Torments in Hell*: "Indeed there was contrition in his heart, but he despaired of the Grace of God, it seeming to him an impossibility to gain God's favor: like unto Cain, who also despaired, saying his sins were greater than could be forgiven him. It was the same with Judas." Faustus then asked to know what was hell? The spirit tells him that "…the mortal soul is such that all thy speculations can never comprehend Hell, nor canst thou conceive the manner of place where the Wrath of God is stored. The origin and structure is God's Wrath, and it hath many titles and designations, as: House of Shame, Abyss, Gullet, Pit, also Dissensio. Fo the souls of the damned are also shamed, scorned and mocked by God and his Blessed Ones...." "Naught may be found there but fumes, fire and the stench of sulphur." "The pit of Hell, like womb of woman, and earth's belly, is never sated." "We spirits shall be free. We have hope of being saved. But the damned will lament the insufferable cold, the unquenchable fire, the unbearable darkness, stench, the aspect of the Devils, and eternal loss of anything good.... They will devour their tongues for great pain. They will wish for death, would gladly die, but cannot...." And they will never be saved, for if they were to have that hope, that hope would encourage and comfort them. "They can have no more hope for salvation than can they hope for a twinkling light in Hell's darkness, for refreshment with drink of water...." Then he tells how kings lament that they had lived for violence, how a rich man wished he had not been miserly, how a lecher wished he had not fornicated, and gluttons and drunkards regret their excesses. And so on. No grace of God shall ever touch these. "They will lie in Hell like unto the bones of the dead... Their firm belief and faith in God—oh they will at last acquire it—will go unheeded and no thought will be taken of them." Faustus was melancholy but his heart was hardened.

Here Followeth The Second Part: Adventures and Sundry Questions

XII: *His Almanacs and Horoscopes*: Faustus horoscopes were famed for their correctness. He served great lords and princes. His tables and almanacs were praised likewise, "... because he set down naught in them but what did indeed come to pass." He presaged fogs, wind, snow, precipitation, famine, war, pestilence, etc.

XIII: *A Disputatio, or Inquiry Concerning the Arts of Astronomia or Astrologia*: He asked Mephisto about the nature of astronomia. The spirit replied that ancient stargazers could not forecast with certainty because "... these are deep mysteries of God which mortals cannot plumb as we spirits can, who hover in the ari beneath Heaven where we can see and mark what God has predestined." "... all green inexperienced astrologi have set up their horoscopes arbitrarily according to conjecture."

XIV: *A Disputatio and False Answer Which the Spirit Gave to Doctor Faustus:* Faustus complained that Mephisto was not truly his obedient servant: "I cannot have my will of thee." But Mephisto said he had always "humored" him and only once withheld information (that is, the nature of heaven where he cannot go.) Faustus now wondered how God created the World and how mankind was born. "The spirit now gave Faustus a godless, unchristian and childish account." He told him the world has never been born but has always existed and will never cease. "The earth subsists, as always, of itself." The earth and sea created all else harmoniously, but defered to God the creation of mankind and heaven. "…and this is the way they finally became subservient to God." So the spirit tells Faustus that the four elements arose from one realm.

XV: *How Faustus Traveled Down to Hell:* In the eighth year Faustus dreamt of Hell and demanded that his spirit bring forth Belial, but instead Beelzebub appeared. He agreed to take him to Hell. At midnight he came with a "bone chair" upon his back and Faustus sat in it and they flew off. Faustus in fact was asleep but he saw first a volcano on an island, and they swooped into its abyss. He saw flames everywhere but did not feel the heat; he heard sweet music but saw no instruments. He was joined in flight with dragons; a great stag almost toppled him into the abysss but the dragons chased it away. He landed amongst a great multitude of snakes and flying lions came to his aid. They went down further and an angry bull charged at him, and knocekd him out of his chair, but an old ape caught him as he fell and set him in a coach drawn by dragons. They plunged deeper and entered a "great turbid body of water" and submerged. He went deeper and deeper into the terror of the water but at last found himself on a high pointed crag. "He thought to himself: What shalt thou do now, being forasken even by the spirits of Hell? Why thou must hurl thyself either into the water or into the abyss. At this thought he fell into a rage, and in a mad, crazy despair he lept intot he fiery hole, calling out as he cast himself in: Now, spirits, accept my offering. I have earned it. My soul hath caused it." He came to the bottom of hell. Many thousands of knights and men at arms were bathing in a cold river to escape the heat or fleeing from it to the flames in order to be warm. He wanted to take one of the damned by the hand and lead him away but the heat was too

154

great. Beelzebub reappeared with the chair on his back and they flew back. He awoke the next morning in his bed wondering if all he had seen was true and came to believe that it was not, that "the Devil had charmed a vision before his eyes." But this tale was written down and discovered after his death.

XVI: *How Doctor Faustus Journeyed Up into the Stars*: "This record was also found among his possessions." By a general letter Faustus narrates his "ascension into Heaven, among the stars." "One night I could not go to sleep, but lay thinking about my almanacs and horoscopes and about the properties and arrangements in the Heavens, how man--or some of the physics--hath measured those ornaments and would interpret them, even though he cannot really visualize such things and must hence base his interpretations and calculations quite arbitrarily on books and the tenets in them. While in such thoughts, I heard a loud blast of wind go against my house. It threw open my shutters, my chamber door and all else, so that I was not a little astonished. Right afterward I heard a roaring voice saying: Get thee up! Thy heart's desire, intent and lust shalt thou see.... I saw a coach with two dragons come flying down. The coach was illuminated with the flames of Hell, and inasmuch as the moon shone in the sky that night, I could see my steeds as well.... So I climbed up onto my casement, jumped down into my carriage, and off I went, the flying dragons drawing me ever upward.... The higher I ascended, the darker did the world become, and when I would look down into the world from the Heavens above, it was exactly as if I were gazing into a dark hole from bright daylight."

XVII: *Now Will I Tell You What I Did See*: "Departing on a Tuesday, and returning on a Tuesday, I was out one week, during which time I neither slept nor did feel any sleep in me. Incidentally, I remained quite invisible throughout the journey.... I discovered that I could look down upon the world and make out many kingdoms, principalities and seas. I could discern the worlds of Asia, Africa and Europe."

"I observed how it was raining at one place, thundering at another, how the hail did fall here while at another place the weather was fair. In fine, I saw all things in the world as they do usually come to pass....

After I had been up there for a week, I began to observe what was above me, watching from a distance how the Heavens did move and roll around so fast that they seemed about to fly asunder into many thousand pieces, the cloud sphere cracking so violently as if it were about to burst and break the world open. The Heavens were so bright that I could not perceive anything any higher up, and it was so hot that I should have burned to a crisp had my servant not charmed a breeze up for me. The cloud sphere which we see down there in the world is as solid and thick as a masonry wall, but it is of one piece and as clear as crystal. The rain, which originates there and then falls upon the earth, is so clear that we could see ourselves reflected in it....

Down in our world it doth appear and I thought so, too—that the sun is no bigger than the head of a barrel. But it is in fact much bigger than the whole world: for I could discover no end to it at all. At night, when the sun goeth down, the moon must take on the sun's light, this being why the moon shineth so bright at night. And directly beneath Heaven there is so much light that even at night it is daytime in Heaven --this even though the earth remaineth quite dark. Thus I saw more than I had desired. One of the stars, for example, was larger than half the world. A planet is as large as the world. And, in the aery sphere, there I beheld the spirits which dwell beneath Heaven.

While descending, I did look down upon the world again, and it was no bigger than the yolk of an egg. Why, to me the world seemed scarcely a span long, but the oceans looked to be twice that size. Thus, on the evening of the seventh day did I arrive home again, and I slept for three days on a row. I have disposed my almanacs and horoscopes in accordance with my observations, and I did not wish to withhold this fact from you. Now inspect your books and see whether the matter is not in accordance with my vision.

And accept my cordial greetings,

Dr. Faustus The astroseer.

XVIII: *Doctor Faustus Third Journey*: He journeyed invisible to
Rome and went unseen into the Pope's palace. "Doctor
Faustus found all there to be his ilk in arrogance, pride, much
insolence, gluttony, drunkenness, whoring, adultery, and other
fine blessings of the Pope and his rabble." "Methought I
were the Devil's own swine, but he will let me fatten for a
long while yet. These swine in Rome are already fatted and
ready to roast and boil." He entertained himself by his
invisibility there: he teased the Pope, blowing into his face as
he supped, so that the Pope would cross himself. He stole the
Popes food and drink and other things. Then he went to
Constantinople and the Turkish Emperor. He caused a a
great fire to appear and confound him and out of it he himself
emerged dressed in the "ornaments and trappings of a Pope."
He said to the Emperor: "Hail Emperor, so full of grace that
I, thy Mahomet do appear unto thee." Then he disappeared
and the Emperor prostrated himself. Faustus returned the
next day in this guise as Mahomet and the Turks worshiped
him and he lay with all the Emperors wives; at last he left
them, ascending into the sky dressed "in papish raiment."

XIX: *Concerning the Stars*: Faustus tells a visiting scholar how
the earth is tiny in the view from the heavens, that stars are as
large as nations, or than the land itself, and the planets as large
as the world.

XX: *A Question on this Topic*: The scholar then asked about
the reality of spirits, which are said to populate the air.
Faustus describes how they move beneath the cloud sphere
("…for they are granted no affinity with the sun"). "It
followeth therefore that the spirits, not being able to endure
or to suffer the aspect of the sun… must come near to us on
earth and dwell with men, frightening them with nightmares,
howling and spooks."

XXI: *The Second Question*: The scholar then asks about the
luminance of the stars. Faustus tells him that there are three
spheres of heaven and the stars are in the first two nearest the
earth. "Night, observed from Heaven, is nothing else than
day…"

XXII: *The Third Question.* The scholar repeats his questions concerning the make-up of stars and why they fall. Faustus says that they do not really fall. "… this is nothing more than a fancy of mankind. When by night a great streak of fire is seen to shoot downward, these are not falling stars, although we do call them that, but only slaggy pieces from the stars." "But it is my opinion that no star itself falleth except as a scourge of God. Then such stars bring a murkiness of the Heavens with them and cause great floods and devastation of lives and land."

Here Followeth the Third Part, Doctor Faustus: His Adventure: the Things He Performed and Worked with His Nigromantia at the Courts of Great Potentates

XXIII: *A History of the Emperor Charles V and Doctor Faustus*: Seeing Faustus at one of his audiences, the Emperor asked the doctor to prove his ability for nigromantia. He asked Faustus to manifest Alexander the Great and his spouse. "Presently Emperor Alexander entered in the very form which he had borne in life—namely: a well-proportioned, stout little man with a red or red-blond, thick beard, ruddy cheeks…" Alexander bowed the Emperor and so likewise did his spouse. But the Emperor doubted the apparition and said for further proof he must see the birthmark that she had on her backside. She lifted her skirt and proved herself.

XXIV: *Concerning the Antlers of a Hart*: Mephisto charmed a hart's antlers on the head of a sleeping knight at the Emperor's court, as he he lay asleep with his head upon the window sill; the antlers going out of the window, being too large to draw within, the knight was caught when he awoke. Faustus released the spell.

XXV: *Concerning Three Lords who were Rapidly Transported to the Royal Wedding in Munich*: Three students of Wittemberg were tardy for a wedding in Munich for the son of the Duke of Bavaria. The decided to pay Faustus for services of aerial transport. On the day in question he bade the three stand upon his cloak that he had laid out in his garden and with his "coniurationes" a wind arose and lifted the cloak and the three of them and flew them to Munich. They arrived invisibly and appeared in the banqquet hall in time for the meal. Faustus warned them not to speak but the Duke of Bavaria engaged them. When they spoke Faustus called out "up and away!" and the three were supposed to grab the cloak for its flight home. But one failed and was taken prisoner. Faustus employed his magic in person to unlock his gaol and return him to Wittemberg.

XXVI: *Concerning an Adventure with a Jew*: In the fourth year of the pact Faustus was told to use his own magic and wits to gain wealth. He borrowed money from a Jew. Faustus refused to repay him. When he came to house to demand payment, Faustus offered to amputate his arm or leg as a "pawn." "The Jew (for Jews are enemies to us Christians, anyhow) pondered the matter and concluded that it must be a right reckless man who would place his limbs in pawn. But still he accepted it." Faustus took a saw and cut off his leg. The jew took it away but had second thoughts, thinking it would rot and anyway Faustus could not put it on again, so he threw into a river as he crossed over it by bridge. Three days later Faustus would settle the debt in cash but the Jew not having the leg was obliged to forfeit the debt without any payment because he could not return the leg.

XXVII: *An Adventure at the Court of the Count of Anhalt*: Faustus was invited to dine with the Count of Anhalt and seeing that his wife was pregnant, he offered to conjure her anything she might wish to eat. At her behest he brought forth a silver bowl of white and red grapes, and another of green apples and pears. Faustus explained that these came from the Orient where it was yet summer while it was winter in the Occident. "...for the heavens are round." "The sun hath even now betaken himself beneath the earth, and it is night; but in this same instant the sun doth run the earth there, and they shall have day...."

XXVIII: *The Manner in Which Doctor Faustus as Bacchus Kept Shrovetide*: He returned to Wittemberg as Shrovetide approached. Faustus played Bacchus and by magic took the crowd of students and himself to the cellars of the Bishop of Salzburg. "Here they tasted all sorts of wine, for the Bishop hath a glorious grpae culture...." Being discovered byt the Bishop's butler as theives, Faustus conjured them all back by flight, and dropped the poor butler in a tree along the way. In the following morning, the butler, still perched in the pinnacle of that tree, was discovered by peasants, who could not fathom how he got there, but reported it to authorities.

XXIX: *Concerning Helen, Charmed Out of Greece*: On Whitsunday gathering for dinner at Faustus, the students discussed beautiful women and one opined that Helen of Troy must be the loveliest of all. "Forbidding that any should speak or arise from table to receive her, Faustus went out of the parlor and, coming in again, was followed at the heel by Queen Helen." She had the trademark beauty of the Germanic fairy tale or Celtic tradition: coal-black eyes, lips as red as cherries, small mouth, neck like a white swan, glorious golden hair. "...when they went to bed they could not sleep for thinking of the figure and form which had appeared visibly before them, and from this we may learn how the Devil doth blind men with love—oh it doth often happen that a man goeth awhoring for so long that at last he can no longer be saved from it."

XXX: *Concerning a Gesticulation Involving Four Wheels*: Faustus was brought to Brunswick to cure a marshall of consumption. On his way into the town he asked to get a ride in the cart of a passing peasant who refused him. In anger Faustus used his magic to separate the wheels from the cart and they floated away to four different gates of the city. The horses fell down as if dead. The peasant now begged Faustus to forgive him. "Doctor Faustus took pity upon the clown's humility and answered him, saying that must treat no one else in this had manner, there being nothing more shameful than the qualities of churlishness and misanthropy...." He revived the horses and told the man where to find his wheels.

XXXI: *Concerning Four Sorcerers Who Cut Off One Another's Heads and Put Them On Again, Wherein Doctor Faustus, Attending Their Performance, Doth Play the Major Role*: At a carnival in Frankfurt, Faustus attended a demonstration by four sorcerers at an inn in Jews Alley. The four would cut off their heads.

"...he found the sorcerers just getting ready to chop off their heads, and with them was a barber who was going to trim and wash them. Upon a table they had a glass cruse with distilled water in it. One among them, the chief sorcerer and

also their executioner, laid his hands
upon the first of his fellows and charmed
a lily into this cruse. It waxed green, and
he called it the Root of Life. Now he
beheaded that first fellow, let the barber
dress the head, then set it upon the
man's shoulders again. In one and the
same instant, the lily disappeared and the
man was whole again. This was done
with the second and the third sorcerer in
like manner. A lily was charmed for each
in the water, they were executed, their
heads were then dressed and put back on
them again. He called it the Root of Life.
At last it was the turn of the chief
sorcerer and executioner. His Root of
Life was blooming away in the water and
waxing green, now his head was smitten
off also, and they set to washing it and
dressing it in Faustus' presence, which
sorcery did sorely vex him: the arrogance
of this *magicus princeps,* how he let his
head be chopped off so insolently, with
blasphemy and laughter in his mouth.
Doctor Faustus went up to the table
where the cruse and the flowering lily
stood, took out his knife, and snipped
the flower, severing the stem. No one
was aware of this at the time, but when
the sorcerers sought to set the head on
again their medium was gone, and the
evil fellow had to perish with his sins
upon his severed head."

XXXII: *Concerning an Old Man Who Would Have Converted Doctor
Faustus from His Godless Life:* A "Christian, pious, god-fearing
physician" was a neighbor of Faustus and knew of his
"mischief, but he also knew that the time was not yet ripe for
the civil authorities to establish these facts." He invited
Faustus to dine and prostelyzed him: "I beg you my Lord,
take my plea ot your heart, ask God for pardon for Christ's
sake, and abjure at the same time your evil practices, for
sorcery is against God and His Commandment...." Faustus
went home and soberly considered these words but the spirit

Mephisto appeared: "The Devil hath the power (he spake) to fetch thee away. I am in fact now come with the command to dispose of thee—or to obtain thy promise that thou wilt never allow thyself to be seduced, and that thou wilt consign thyself anew with thy blood. Thou must declare immediately what thou wouldst do, or I am to slay thee."

XXXIII: *Pact*: A second pact follows. Again he pledges in blood, his body and soul: "Now therefore do I further promise him that I will never more heed the admonitions, teachings, scoldings, instructions or threats of mankind, neither as concernth the Word of God nor in any temporal or spiritual matters whatsoever...." Faustus then hated his neighbor, the goodly physician, and conspired to kill him. Two days later as the good man was going to bed he heard a rumbling in his house. A spirit came into his chamber, "grunting like a sow." The good man mocked the spirit and drove it away. "Thus doth God protect all good Christians who seek in Him succor against the Evil One."

Doctor Faustus: His Last Tricks and What He Did in the Final Years of His Contract:

XXXIV: *How Doctor Faustus Brought About the Marriage of Two Lovers*: A student of Faustus, one N. Reuckauer, loved a young woman and pined away for her sake. Faustus offered to help him win her affections. Faustus employed his sorcery to "disturb her heart." Later at her house, Reuckauer was to ask her to dance with him, as Faustus directed him to do, and that he should touch her with a magic ring and she should love him. "Now he took some distilled water and washed Reuckauer with it, so that his face presently became exceedingly handsome. Reuckauer followed Faustus' instructions carefully..." She was "pierced through with Cupid's arrow." They married upon her ardent entreaty, as Faustus had predicted.

XXXV: *Concerning Divers Flora in Doctor Faustus's Garden on Christmas Day*: Invited to Christmas dinner, several gentlewomen reported, as they trudged thru the winter's snow to his house, seeing in his garden no snow at all but a summery complexion and vines growing with grapes, and roses blooming and smelling sweetly.

162

XXXVI: *Concerning an Army Raised Against My Lord of Hardeck*: The knight who had been charmed with hart antlers chanced upon Faustus one day while out riding with some of his men. They charged him but upon catching up with him, over the rise of a hill, a counter-offensive of some hundred phantom cavalry came after them. Wherever they went yet another troop of calvary surprised them. Faustus then approached and bade them surrender. He took away their horses and musket, and gave them enchanted ones in their stead. They returned to their castle but when the horses were rode into water they disappeared and the men nearly drowned. Faustus in the meantime sold the knights horses for a good profit.

XXXVII: *Concerning the Beautiful Helen from Greece, How She Lived for a Time with Doctor Faustus*: Towards the end of the twenty-second year of the pact, Faustus desired Helen of Greece to be his concubine. This done, she bore him a son, whom was named Justus Faustus. None heard of either again after Faustus died.

XXXVIII: *Concerning One Whose Wife Married While He Was Captive in Turkey, and How Doctor Faustus Informed and Aided Him*: Johann Werner of Reuttpueffel had gone to school with Faustus. He went to Turkey and Holy Lands and disappeared. After three years his wife gave up hope of him and married another man. Faustus asked Mephisto whether Werner was still alive and was the spirit answered yes. Faustus then charmed the rival husband so that he could not consummate the marriage, and was impotent: "This did cause the lady to grieve and to think on her precious husband whom she thought to be dead, for he had rightly known how to tousle her." Meanwhile, Faustus saw to Werner's release and he returned to his wife.

XXXIX: *Concerning the Testatment: What Doctor Faustus Bequethed His Servant Christoph Wagner*: "Wagner was a wicked and dissipated knave who had gone about begging in Wittemberg but had found no kindness with anyone until he had met Faustus…." Faustus bequeathed him his house, money and other possessions which he had gained by his sorcery.

XL: *The Discourse Which Doctor Faustus Held with His Son Concerning the Testament*: He gave his son his books. Three days later he asked Wagner if he wanted a spirit to serve hiim as Mephisto had served him. Wagner said he wanted one In the guise of an ape. One immediately so appeared.

XLI: *What Doctor Faustus Did in the Final Month of His Pact*: "His days ran out like the sand in an hourglass, and when only one month remained of the twenty-four years which he had contracted of the Devil (as we have read) Doctor Faustus became fainthearted, depressed, deeply melancholic, like unto an imprisoned murderer and highwayman over whose head the sentence hath been pronounced and who now in the dungeon awaiteth punishment and death."

XLII: *Doctor Faustus His Lamentation, that He Must Die at a Yoiiung and a Lusty Age*: "Alas, Reason and Free Will! What a heavy charge ye do level at these limbs…. Alas ye limbs, and thou yet whole body! It was yet let Reason indict Soul, for I might have chosen succor for my soul by sacrificing thee, my body."

XLIII: *Doctor Faustus Lamenteth Yet Further.* "Alas, Worldly Pleasure! Into what wretchedness hast thou led me, darkening and blinding my eyes…. Where am I to hide?"

XLIV: *Doctor Faustus His Hideous End and Spectaculum*: Faustus invited his students to his home for one last dinner. He addressed them: "An hourglass standeth before mine eyes and I watch for it to finish. I know the Devil will have his due." "Now let this my hideous end be an example unto you so long as ye many live, and a remembrance to love God and to entreat Him to protect you from the guile and deceit of the Devil…." "He tried to pray, but he could not. As it was with Cain, who said his sins were greater than could be forgiven, so was it with Faustus also, who was convinced that in making his written contract with the Devil he had gone to far."

At midnight a wind stormed against the house. "…over the raging of the wind they heard a hideous music, as if snakes, adders and other serpents were in the house. Doctor Faustus' door creaked open. There then arose a crying out of Murther! And Help! But the voice was weak and hollow, soon dying out entirely. When it was day the students, who had not slept this entire night, went into the chamber where Doctor Faustus had lain, but they found no Faustus there. The parlor was full of blood. Brain clave unto the walls where the Fiend had dashed

164

him from one to the other. Here lay his eyes, here a few teeth. O it was a hideous *spectaculum*. Then began the students to bewail and beweep him, seeking him in many places. When they came out to the dung heap, here they found his corpse. It was monstrous to behold, for head and limbs were still twitching. These students and magisters who were present at Faustus' death gained permission afterwards to bury him in the village. Subsequently, they retired to his domicile where they found the famulus Wagner already mourning his master. This little book, *Doctor Faustus His Historia,* was already all written out. Now as to what his famulus wrote, that will be a different, new book. On this same day the enchanted Helen and her son Justus Faustus were also gone. So uncanny did it become in Faustus' house that none could dwell there. Doctor Faustus himself walked about at night, making revelations unto Wagner as regardeth many secret matters. Passers-by reported seeing his face peering out at the windows."

166

Excerpts of English Faustbook of 1592

IOhn Faustus, borne in the town of *Rhode,* lying in the Prouince
of *Weimer* in *Germ[anie,]* his father a poore Husbandman, and
not [able] wel to bring him vp: but hauing an Vncle at
Wittenberg, a rich man, & without issue, took this *I. Faustus*
from his father, & made him his heire, in so much that his
father was no more troubled with him, for he remained with
his Vncle at *Wittenberg,* where he was kept at y Vniuersitie in
the same citie to study diuinity. But *Faustus* being of a naughty
minde & otherwise addicted, applied not his studies, but tooke
himselfe to other exercises: the which his Vncle oftentimes
hearing, rebuked him for it, as *Eli* oft times rebuked his
children for sinning against the Lord: euen so this good man
laboured to haue *Faustus* apply his study of Diuinitie, that he
might come to the knowledge of God & his lawes. But it is
manifest that many vertuous parents haue wicked children, as
Cayn, Ruben, Absolom, and such like haue béen to their parents:
so this *Faustus* hauing godly parents, and seeing him to be of a
toward wit, were very desirous to bring him vp in those
vertuous studies, namely, of Diuinitie: but he gaue himself
secretly to study Necromancy and Coniuration, in so much
that few or none could perceiue his profession.

But to the purpose: *Faustus* continued at study in the
Vniuersity, & was by the Rectors and sixteene Masters after
wards examined howe he had profited in his studies; and
being found by them, that none for his time were able to
argue with him in Diuinity, or for the excellency of his
wisedome to compare with him, with one consent they made
him Doctor of Diuinitie. But Doctor *Faustus* within short time
after hee had obtayned his degree, fell into such fantasies and
deepe cogitations, that he was marked of many, and of the
most part of the Students was called the *Speculator,* and
sometime he would throw the Scriptures from him as though
he had no care of his former profession: so that hee began a
very vngodly life, as hereafter more at large may appeare; for
the olde Prouerb sayth, Who can hold that wil away? so, who
can hold *Faustus* from the diuel, that seekes after him with al
his indeuour ': For he accompanied himselfe with diuers that
were séene In those diuelish Arts, and that had the *Chaldean,
Persian, Hebrew, Arabian,* and *Greeke* tongues, vsing Figures,
characters, Coniurations, Incantations, with many other
ceremonies belonging to these infernal Arts as Necromancie,

168

Charmes, South-saying, Witchcraft, Inchantment, being
delighted with their bookes, words, and names so well, that he
studied day and night therein: in so much that hee could not
abide to bee called Doctor of Diuinitie, but waxed a worldly
man, and named himselfe an Astrologian, and a
Mathematician: & for a shadow sometimes a Phisitian, and did
great cures, namely, with hearbs, rootes, waters, drinks,
receipts, & clisters. And without doubt he was passing wise,
and excellent perfect in the holy scriptures: but hee that
knoweth his masters will and doth it not, is worthy to be
beaten with many stripes. It is written, no man can serue two
masters: and, thou shalt not tempt the Lord thy God: but
Faustus threw all this in the winde, & made his soule of no
estimation, regarding more his worldly pleasure than ye ioyes
to come: therfore at ye day of iudgement there is no hope of
his redemptio.

----

* Rhode: 'Rhode,' modern Roda, about thirty
kilometers southeast of Weimar.
* Rhode: Illegible in the British Museum copy
(hereafter referred to as B.M.).
* [able]: Illegible in B.M.
* ben: The reason for the accent is not clear. It occurs
in the text only where ee is printed as a ligature.
* a toward wit: an apt or willing mind
* : The paging of B.M. is indicated in the brackets.
There are frequent errors in pagination.
* ':: B.M. uses two types of interrogation point, viz., ':
and ? The difference in significance is not clear. See
McKerrow, *Introduction to Bibliography*, Oxford, 1927,
p. 316.
* sene: versed in
* for a shadow: as a blind
* clisters: enemas

*How Doctor Faustus began to practise in his diuelish Arte, and how he
coniured the Diuel, making him to appeare and meete him on the morrow
at his owne house. Chap. 2*

YOu haue heard before, that all *Faustus* minde was set to study the artes of Necromancie and Coniuration, the which exercise hee followed day and night: and taking to him the wings of an Eagle, thought to flie ouer the whole world, and to know the secrets of heauen and earth; for his Speculation was so wonderfull, being expert in vsing his *Vocabula*, Figures, Characters, Coniurations, and other Ceremoniall actions, that in all the haste hee put in practise to bring the Diuell before him. And taking his way to a thicke Wood neere to *Wittenberg*, called in the Germane tongue *Spisser Waldt*: that is in English the *Spissers Wood*, (as *Faustus* would oftentimes boast of it among his crue being in his iolitie,) he came into the same wood towards euening into a crosse way, where he made with a wand a Circle in the dust, and within that many more Circles and Characters: and thus he past away the time, vntill it was nine or ten of the clocke in the night, then began Doctor *Faustus* to call for *Mephostophiles* the Spirite, and to charge him in the name of *Beelzebub* to appeare there personally without any long stay: then presently the Diuel began so great a rumor in the Wood, as if heauen and earth would haue come together with winde, the trees bowing their tops to the ground, then fell the Diuell to bleare as if the whole Wood had been full of Lyons, and sodainly about the Circle ranne the Diuell as if a thousand Wagons had been running together on paued stones. After this at the foure corners of the Wood it thundred horribly, with such lightnings as if the whole worlde, to his seeming, had been on fire. *Faustus* all this while halfe amazed at the Diuels so long tarrying, and doubting whether he were best to abide any more such horrible Coniurings, thought to leaue his Circle and depart; wherevpon the Diuel made him such musick of all sortes, as if the Nimphes themselues had beene in place: whereat *Faustus* was reuiued and stoode stoutly in his Circle aspecting his purpose, and began againe to coniure the spirite *Mephostophiles* in the name of the Prince of Diuels to appeare in his likenesse: where at sodainly ouer his head hanged houering in the ayre a mighty Dragon: then cals *Faustus* againe after his Diuelish maner, at which there was a monstrous crie in the Wood, as if hell had been open, and all the tormented soules crying to God for mercy; presently not three fadome aboue his head fell a flame in manner of a lightning, and changed it selfe into a Globe: yet *Faustus* feared it not, but did perswade himselfe that the Diuell should giue him his request before hee would leaue: Oftentimes after to his companions he would boast,

170

that he had the stoutest head (vnder the cope of heauen) at commandement: whereat they answered, they knew none stouter than the Pope or Emperour: but Doctor *Faustus* said, the head that is my seruant is aboue all on earth, and repeated certain wordes out of Saint *Paul* to the *Ephesians* to make his argument good: The Prince of this world is vpon earth and vnder heauen. Wel, let vs come againe to his Coniuration where we left him at his fiery Globe: *Faustus* vexed at the Spirits so long tarying, vsed his Charmes with full purpose not to depart before he had his intent, and crying on *Mephostophiles* the Spirit; sodainly the Globe opened and sprang vp in height of a man: so burning a time, in the end it conuerted to the shape of a fiery man. This pleasant beast ranne about the circle a great while, and lastly appeared in manner of a gray Frier, asking *Faustus* what was his request. *Faustus* commaunded that the next morning at twelue of the clocke hee should appeare to him at his house; but the diuel would in no wise graunt: [page 5] *Faustus* began againe to coniure him in the name of *Beelzebub*, that he should fulfil his request: whereupon the Spirit agreed, and so they departed each one his way.

----

* Vocabula: magic words
* rumor: uproar
* bleare: roar
* aspecting his purpose: keeping in mind his object

The conference of Doctor Faustus with the Spirit Mephostophiles the morning following at his owne house. Chap. 3

DOctor *Faustus* hauing commaunded the Spirit to be with him, at his houre appointed he came and appeared in his chamber, demanding of *Faustus* what his desire was: then began Doctor *Faustus* anew with him to coniure him that he should be obedient vnto him, & to answere him certaine Articles, and to fulfil them in al points.

1.   That the Spirit should serue him and be obedient vnto him in all things that he asked of him from yt houre vntil the houre of his death.

2.   Farther, any thing that he desired of him he should bring it to him.

3.   Also, that in all *Faustus* his demaunds or Interrogations, the spirit should tell him nothing but that which is true.

Hereupon the Spirit answered and laid his case foorth, that he had no such power of himselfe, vntil he had first giuen his Prince (that was ruler ouer him) to vnderstand thereof, and to know if he could obtaine so much of his Lord: therfore speake farther that I may do thy whole desire to my Prince: for it is not in my power to fulfill without his leaue. Shew me the cause why (said *Faustus*.) The Spirit answered: *Faustus*, thou shalt vnderstand, that with vs it is euen as well a kingdome, as with you on earth: yea, we haue our rulers and seruants, as I my selfe am one, and we name our whole number the Legion: for although that *Lucifer* is thrust and falle out of heauen through his pride and high minde, yet he hath notwithstanding a Legion of Diuels at his commaundement, that we call the *Oriental* Princes; for his power is great and infinite. Also there is an host in *Meridie*, in *Septentrio*, in *Occidente*: and for that *Lucifer* hath his kingdome vnder heauen, wee must change and giue our selues vnto men to serue them at their pleasure. It is also certaine, we haue neuer as yet opened vnto any man the truth of our dwelling, neither of our ruling, neither what our power is, neither haue we giuen any man any gift, or learned him any thing, except he promise to be ours.

Doctor *Faustus* vpon this arose where he sate, & said, I wil haue my request, and yet I wil not be damned. The spirit answered, Then shalt thou want thy desire, & yet art thou mine notwithstanding: if any man would detaine thee it is in vain, for thine infidelity hath confouded thée.

Hereupon spake *Faustus*: Get thee hence from me, and take Saint *Valentines* farewell & *Crisam* with thee, yet I coniure thee that thou be here at euening, and bethinke thy selfe on that I haue asked thee, and aske thy Princes counsel therein.

Mephostophiles the Spirit, thus answered, vanished away, leauing *Faustus* in his study, where he sate pondering with himselfe how he might obtaine his request of the diuel without losse of his soule: yet fully he was resolued in himselfe, rather than to want his pleasure, to doe whatsoeuer the Spirit and his Lord should condition vpon.

> * host in Meridie: 'Host' is a mistranslation of the German 'Herrschaft,' kingdom. 'Meridie' is south; 'Septentrio,' north; 'Occidente,' west.
> * Saint Valentines farewell Crisam with thee: 'Saint Valentines farewell & Crisam with thee' is about equivalent to 'a pest upon you.' Logeman, *English Faustbook of 1592*, p. 137, gives a discussion of the derivation of the phrase.

The second time of the Spirits appearing to Faustus in his house, and of their parley. Chap. 4.

FAustus continuing in his diuelish cogitations, neuer mouing out of the place where the Spirit left him (such was his feruent loue to the diuel) the night approching, this swift flying Spirit appeared to *Faustus*, offering himself with al submissiô to his seruice, with ful authority from his Prince to doe whatsoeuer he would request, if so be *Faustus* would promise to be his: this answere I bring thee, and an answere must thou make by me againe, yet will I heare what is thy desire, because thou hast sworne me to be here at this time. Doctor *Faustus* gaue him this answere, though faintly (for his soules sake) That his request was none other but to become a Diuel, or at the least a limme of him, and that the Spirit should agree vnto these Articles as followeth.

1.   That he might be a Spirite in shape and qualitie.

2.   That *Mephostophiles* should be his seruant, and at his commandement.

3.   That *Mephostophiles* should bring him any thing, and doo for him whatsoeuer.

4.   That at all times he should be in his house, inuisible to all men, except onely to himselfe, and at his commandement to shew himselfe.

5.   Lastly, that *Mephostophiles* should at all times appeare at his command, in what forme or shape soeuer he would.

Vpon these poynts the Spirit answered Doctor *Faustus*, that

all this should be granted him and fulfilled, and more if he would agree vnto him vpon certaine Articles as followeth.

First, that Doctor *Faustus* should giue himselfe to his Lord *Lucifer*, body and soule.

Secondly, for confirmation of the same, he should make him a writing, written with his owne blood.

Thirdly, that he would be an enemie to all Christian people.

Fourthly, that he would denie his Christian beleefe.

Fiftly, that he let not any man change his opinion, if so bee any man should goe about to disswade, or withdraw him from it.

Further, the spirit promised *Faustus* to giue him certaine yeares to liue in health and pleasure, and when such yeares were expired, that then *Faustus* should be fetched away, and if he should holde these Articles and conditions, that then he should haue all whatsoeuer his heart would wish or desire; and that *Faustus* should quickly perceiue himself to be a Spirit in all maner of actions whatsoeuer. Hereupon Doctor *Faustus* his minde was so inflamed, that he forgot his soule, and promised *Mephostophiles* to hold all things as hee had mentioned them: he thought the diuel was not so black as they vse to paynt him, nor hell so hote as the people say, &c.

174

The third parley between Doctor Faustus and Mephostophiles about a conclusion. Chap. 5.

AFter Doctor *Faustus* had made his promise to the diuell, in the morning betimes he called the Spirit before him and commaunded him that he should alwayes come to him like a Fryer, after the order of Saint *Francis*, with a bell in his hande like Saint *Anthonie*, and to ring it once or twise before he appeared, that he might know of his certaine comming:

Then *Faustus* demaunded the Spirit, what was his name? The Spirit answered, my name is as thou sayest, *Mephostophiles*, and I am a prince, but seruant to *Lucifer*: and all the circuit from *Septentrio* to the *Meridian*, I rule vnder him. Euen at these words was this wicked wretch *Faustus* inflamed, to heare himselfe to haue gotten so great a Potentate to be his seruant, forgot the Lord his maker, and Christ his redeemer, became an enemy vnto all man-kinde, yea, worse than the Gyants whom the Poets fayne to climb the hilles to make warre with the Gods: not vnlike that enemy of God and his Christ, that for his pride was cast into hell: so likewise *Faustus* forgot that the high climbers catch the greatest falles, and that the sweetest meate requires the sowrest sawce.

After a while, *Faustus* promised *Mephostophiles* to write and make his Obligation, with full assurance of the Articles in the Chapter before rehearsed. A pitifull case, (Christian Reader,) for certainly this Letter or Obligation was found in his house after his most lamentable end, with all the rest of his damnable practises vsed in his whole life. Therefore I wish al Christians to take an example by this wicked *Faustus*, and to be comforted in Christ, contenting themselues with that vocation whereunto it hath pleased God to call them, and not to esteeme the vaine delights of this life, as did this vnhappie *Faustus*, in giuing his Soule to the Diuell: & to confirme it the more assuredly, he tooke a small penknife, and prickt a vaine in his left hand, & for certaintie therevpon, were seene on his hand these words written, as if they had been written with blood, o homo fuge: whereat the Spirit vanished, but *Faustus* continued in his damnable minde, & made his writing as followeth.

How Doctor Faustus set his blood in a saucer on warme ashes, and writ as followeth. Chap. 6

I *Iohannes Faustus*, Doctor, doe openly acknowledge with mine ownehand, to the greater force and strengthning of this Letter, that siththence I began to studie and speculate the course and order of the Elements, I haue not found through the gift that is giuen mee from aboue, any such learning and wisdome, that can bring mee to my desires: and for that I find, that men are vnable to instruct me any farther in the matter, now haue I Doctor *John Faustus*, vnto the hellish prince of Orient and his messenger *Mephostophiles*, giuen both bodie & soule, vpon such condition, that they shall learne me, and fulfill my desire in all things, as they haue promised and vowed vnto me, with due obedience vnto me, according vnto the Articles mentioned betweene vs.

Further, I couenant and grant with them by these presents, that at the end of 24. yeares next ensuing the date of this present Letter, they being expired, and I in the meane time, during the said yeares be serued of them at my wil, they accomplishing my desires to the full in al points as we are agreed, that then I giue them full power to doe with mee at their pleasure, to rule, to send, fetch, or carrie me or mine, be it either body, soule, flesh, blood, or goods, into their habitation, be it wheresoeuer: and herevpon, I defie God and his Christ, all the hoast of heauen, and all liuing creatures that beare the shape of God, yea all that liues; and againe I say it, and it shall be so. And to the more strengthning of this writing, I haue written it with mine owne hand and blood, being in perfect memory, and herevpon I subscribe to it with my name and title, calling all the infernall, middle, and supreme powers to witnesse of this my Letter and subscription.

Iohn Faustus, approued in the Elements, and the spirituall Doctor.

----

    * approued in the Elements: proved or tested in the
    elements

How Doctor Faustus would haue married, and how the Diuell had almost killed him for it. Chap. 9.

DOctor *Faustus* continued thus in his Epicurish life day & night, and beleeued not that there was a God, hell, or diuel: he thought that bodie and soule died together, and had quite forgotten Diuinitie or the immortalitie of his soule, but stoode in his damnable heresie day and night. And bethinking himselfe of a wife, called *Mephostophiles* to counsaile; which would in no wise agree: demanding of him if he would breake the couenant made with him, or if hee had forgot it. Hast not thou (quoth *Mephostophiles*) sworne thy selfe an enemy to God and all creatures': To this I answere thee, thou canst not marry; thou canst not serue two masters, God, and my Prince: for wedlock is a chiefe institution ordained of God, and that hast thou promised to defie, as we doe all, and that hast thou also done: and moreouer thou hast confirmed it with thy blood: perswade thy selfe, that what thou doost in contempt of wedlock, it is all to thine owne delight. Therefore *Faustus*, looke well about thee, and bethinke thy selfe better, and I wish thee to change thy minde: for if thou keepe not what thou hast promised in thy writing, we wil teare thee in peeces like the dust vnder thy feete. Therefore sweete *Faustus*, thinke with what vnquiet life, anger, strife, & debate thou shalt liue in when thou takest a wifc: therefore change thy minde.

Doctor *Faustus* was with these speeches in despaire: and as all that haue forsaken the Lord, can build vpon no good foundation: so this wreched *Faustus* hauing forsooke the rock, fell in despaire with himself, fearing if he should motion Matrimonie any more, that the diuell would teare him in peeces For this time (quoth he to *Mephostophiles*)

I am not minded to marry. Then you doe well, answered his spirite. But shortly & that within two houres after, *Faustus* called his spirit, which came in his old maner like a Frier. Then *Faustus* said vnto him, I am not able to resist nor bridle my fantasie, I must and will haue a wife, and I pray thee giue thy consent to it. Sodainlie vpon these words came such a

whirle-winde about the place, that *Faustus* thought the whole
house would come down, all the doores in the house flew off
the hookes: after all this, his house was full of smoke, and the
floore couered ouer with ashes: which when Doctor *Faustus*
perceiued, he would haue gone Vp the staires: and flying Vp,
he was taken and throwne into the hall, that he was not able
to stir hand nor foote: then round about him ran a monstrous
circle of fire, neuer standing still, that *Faustus* fried as hee lay,
and thought there to haue been burned. Then cried hee out to
his Spirit *Mephostophiles* for help, promising him hee would liue
in all things as he had vowed in his hand-writing. Hereupon
appeared vnto him an ougly Diuell, so fearefull and
monstrous to beholde, that *Faustus* durst not looke on him.
The Diuell said, what wouldst thou haue *Faustus*: how likest
thou thy wedding? what minde art thou in now': *Faustus*
answered, he had forgot his promise, desiring him of pardon,
and he would talke no more of such things. The diuell
answered, thou were best so to doe, and so vanished.

After appeared vnto him his Frier *Mephostophiles* with a bel in
his hand, and spake to *Faustus*: It is no iesting with vs, holde
thou that which thou hast vowed, and wee will performe as
wee haue promised: and more than that, thou shalt haue thy
hearts desire of what woman soeuer thou wilt, bee shee aliue
or dead, and so long as thou wilt, thou shalt keepe her by thee.

These words pleased *Faustus* wonderfull well, and repented
himselfe that hee was so foolish to wish himselfe married, that
might haue any woman in the whole Citie brought to him at
his command; the which he practised and perseuered in a long
time.

----

* motion: propose
* within: B.M. has 'wihtin.'
* wonderfull: B.M. has 'wonderfnll.'

178

How Doctor Faustus desired to see hell, and of the maner how hee was vsed therein. Chap. 20.

DOctor *Faustus* bethinking how his time went away, and how he had spent eight yeares thereof, he ment to spend the rest to his better contentment, intending quite to forget any such motions as might offend the Diuell any more: wherefore on a time he called his spirit *Mephostophiles*, and said vnto him, bring thou hither vnto mee thy Lord *Lucifer*, or *Belial*: he brought him (notwithstanding) one that was called *Beelzebub*, the which asked *Faustus* his pleasure. Quoth *Faustus*, I would knowe of thee if I may see Hell and take a view thereof: That thou shalt (said the diuell) and at midnight I will fetch thee. Well, night being come, Doctor *Faustus* awaited very diligently for the comming of the Diuell to fetch him, and thinking that hee tarried all too long, he went to the window, where hee pulled open a cazement, and looking into the Element, hee sawe a cloude in the North more black, darke and obscure, than all the rest of the Sky, from whence the winde blew most horrible right into *Faustus* his chamber, filled the whole house with smoake, that *Faustus* was almost smothered: hereat fell an exceeding thunderclap, and withall came a great rugged black Beare, all curled, & vpon his backe a chayre of beaten golde, and spake to *Faustus*, saying, sit vp and away with me: and Doctor *Faustus* that had so long abode the smoake, wisht rather to be in hell than there, got on the Diuell, and so they went together. But marke how the Diuell blinded him, and made him beleeue that he carried him into hell, for he caned him into the ayre, where *Faustus* fell into a sound sleepe, as if hee had sate in a warme water or bath: at last they came to a place which burneth continually with flashing flames of fire and brimstone, whereout issued an exceeding mighty clap of thunder, with so horrible a noyse, that *Faustus* awaked, but the Diuell went forth on his way and caned *Faustus* therinto, yet notwithstanding, howsoeuer it burnt, Doctor *Faustus* felt no more heate, than as it were the glimps of the Sunne in May: there heard he all manner of musicke to welcome him, but sawe none playing on them; it pleased him well, but he durst not aske, for hee was forbidden it before. To meet the Diuel & the guest that came with him, came three other ougly Diuels, the which ran back againe before the Beare to make

them way, against whome there came running an exceeding
great Hart, which would haue thrust *Faustus* out of his chayre,
but being defended by the other three Diuels, the Hart was
put to the repulse: thence going on their way *Faustus* looked,
and beholde there was nothing but Snakes, and all manner of
venemous beastes about him, which were exceeding great,
vnto the which Snakes came many Storks, and swallowed vp
all the whole multitude of Snakes, that they left not one:
which when *Faustus* sawe, he marueiled greatly: but
proceeding further on their hellish voyage, there came forth of
a hollow cliffe an exceeding great flying Bull, the which with
such a force hit *Faustus* his chayre with his head and hornes,
that he turned *Faustus* and his Beare ouer and ouer, so that the
Beare vanished away, whereat *Faustus* began to crie: oh, woe is
mee that euer I came here: for hee thought there to haue been
beguiled of the Diuel, and to make his ende before his time
appointed or conditioned of the Diuel: but shortly came
v[n]to him a monstrous Ape, bidding *Faustus* bee of good
cheare, and said, get vpon me; all the fire in hel seemed to
Faustus to haue been put out, wherevpon followed a
monstrous thick fogge, that hee sawe nothing, but shortly it
seemed to him to waxe cleare, where he saw two great
Dragons fastned to a waggon, into the which the Ape
ascended and set *Faustus* therein; foorth flewe the Dragons
into an exceeding darke cloude, where *Faustus* saw neither
Dragon nor Chariot wherein he sat, and such were the cries of
tormented soules, with mightie thunder-claps and flashing
lightnings about his eares, that poore *Faustus* shooke for feare.
Vpon this came they to a water, stinking and filthie, thick like
mudde, into the which ran the Dragons, sinking vnder with
waggon and all; but *Faustus* felt no water but as it were a small
mist, sauing that the waues beate so sore vpon him, that hee
saw nothing vnder and ouer him but only water, in the which
he lost his Dragons, Ape, and waggon; and sinking yet deeper
and deeper, hee came at last as it were vpon an high Rock,
where the waters parted and left him thereon: but when the
water was gone, it seemed to him hee should there haue ended
his life, for he saw no way but death: the Rocke was as high
from the bottome as Heauen is from the earth: there sate he,
seeing nor hearing any man, and looked euer vpon the Rocke;
at length hee saw a little hole, out of the which issued fire;
thought he, how shall I now doe': I am forsaken of the Diuels,
and they that brought mee hither, here must I either fall to the
bottome, or burne in the fire, or sit still in despaire: with that

180

in his madnesse he gaue a leape into the fierie hole, saying: holde you infernall Hagges, take here this sacrifice as my last ende; the which I iustly haue deserued: vpon this he was entred, and finding himselfe as yet vnburned or touched of the fire, he was the better appayed, but there was so great a noyse as he neuer heard the like before, it passed all the thunder that euer he had heard; & coming down further to the bottome of the Rocke, he sawe a fire, wherein were many worthie and noble personages, as Emperours, Kings, Dukes and Lords, and many thousands more of tormented soules, at the edge of which fire ran a most pleasant, cleare, and coole water to beholde, into the which many tormented soules sprang out of the fire to coole themselues; but b[e]ing so freezing cold, they were constrained to returne againe into the fire, and thus wearied themselues and spent their endles torments out of one labyrinth into another, one while in heate, another while in colde: but *Faustus* standing thus all this while gazing on them that were thus tormented, hee sawe one leaping out of the fire and scriching horriblie, whome he thought to haue knowne, wherefore he would fame haue spoken vnto him, but remembring that hee was forbidden, hee refrained speaking. Then this Diuel that brought him in, came to him againe in likenes of a Beare, with the chayre on his back, and bad him sit vp, for it was time to depart: so *Faustus* got vp, and the Diuel caned him out into the ayre, where he had so sweete musick that hee fell asleepe by the way. His boy *Christopher* being all this while at home, and missing his master so long, thought his master would haue taried and dwelt with the Diuell for euer: but whilest his boy was in these cogitations, his master came home, for the Diuel brought him home fast a sleepe as he sate in his chayre, and so he threw him on his bed, where (being thus left of the Diuel) he lay vntil day. When hee awaked, bee was amazed, like a man that had been in a darke dungeon; musing with himselfe if it were true or false that he had seene hel, or whether he was blinded or not: but he rather perswaded himself that he had been there than otherwise, because he had seene such wonderful things: wherefore he most carefully tooke pen and incke, and wrote those thinges in order as hee had seene: the which writing was afterwards found by his boy in his studie; which afterwards was published to the whole citie of *Wittenberg* in open print, for example to all Christians.

How Doctor Faustus made his iourney thorough the principal and most famous lands in the world. Chap. 22.

DOctor *Faustus* hauing ouer-runne fifteen yeers of his appointed time, he tooke vpon him a iourney, with ful pretencec to see the whole world: and calling his spirit *Mephostophiles* vnto him, he sayd: thou knowest that thou art bound vnto me vpon conditions, to performe and fulfill my desire in all thengs, wherfore my pretence is to visite the whole face of the earth visible & inuisible when it pleaseth me: wherfore, I enioyne and command thee to the same. Whereupon *Mephostophiles* answered, I am ready my Lord at thy command & foorthwith the Spirit changed himselfe into the likenes of a flying horse, saying, *Faustus* sit vp, I am ready. Doctor *Faustus* loftily sate vpon him, & forward they went: *Faustus* came thorough many a land & Prouince...

...

Then he visited the seuen Churches of *Rome*, that were S. *Peters*, S. *Pauls*, S. *Sebastians*, S. *Iohn Lateran*, S. *Laurence*, S. *Mary Magdalen*, and S. *Marie maiora*: then went he [page 36] without the towne, where he saw the conduits of water that runne leuell through hill and dale, bringing water into the town fifteen Italian miles off: other monuments he saw, too many to recite, but amongst the rest he was desirous to see the Popes Pallace, and his maner of seruice at his table, wherefore he and his Spirit made themselues inuisible, and came into the Popes Court, and priuie chamber where he was, there saw he many seruants attendant on his holmes, with many a flattering Sycophant carrying of his meate, and there hee marked the Pope and the manner of his seruice, which hee seeing to bee so vnmeasurable and sumptuous; fie (quoth *Faustus*) why had not the Diuel made a Pope of me? *Faustus* saw notwithstanding in that place those that were like to himselfe, proud, stout, wilfull, gluttons, drunkards, whoremongers, breakers of wedlocke, and followers of all manner of vngodly exercises: wherefore he said to his Spirit, I thought that I had been alone a hogge, or porke of the diuels, but he must beare with me yet a little longer, for these hogs of *Rome* are already

fatned, and fitted to make his roste-meate, the Diuel might
doe well nowe to spit them all and hane them to the fire, and
let him summon the Nunnes to turne the spits: for as none
must confesse the Nunne but the Frier, so none should turne
the rosting Frier but the Nunne. Thus continued *Faustus* three
dayes in the Popes Pallace, and yet had no lust to his meate,
but stood still in the Popes chamber, and saw euery thing
whatsoeuer it was: on a time the Pope would haue a feast
prepared for the Cardinall of *Pauia*, and for his first welcome
the Cardinall was bidden to dinner: and as he sate at meate,
the Pope would euer be blessing and crossing ouer his mouth;
Faustus could suffer it no longer, but vp with his fist and
smote the Pope on the face, and withall he laughed that the
whole house might heare him, yet none of them sawe him nor
knew where he was: the Pope perswaded his company that it
was a damned soule, commanding a Masse presently to be
said for his de liuerie out of Purgatory, which was done: the
Pope sate still at meate, but when the latter messe came in to
the Popes boord, Doctor *Faustus* laid hands thereon saying;
this is mine: & so he took both dish & meate & fled vnto the
Capital or Campadolia, calling his spirit vnto him and said:
come let vs be merry, for thou must fetch me some wine, &
the cup that the Pope drinkes of, & here vpon *monte caual* will
wee make good cheare in spight of the Pope & al his fat abbie
lubbers. His spirit hearing this, departed towards the Popes
chamber, where he found the yet sitting and quaffing:
wherefore he tooke from before the Pope the fairest peece of
plate or drinking goblet, & a flaggon of wine, & brought [page
37] it to *Faustus*; but when the Pope and the rest of his crue
perceiued they were robbed, and knew not after what sort,
they perswaded themselues that it was the damned soule that
before had vexed the Pope so, & that smote him on the face,
wherefore he sent commandement through al the whole Citie
of *Rome*, that they should say Masse in euery Church, and ring
al the bels for to lay the walking Spirit, & to curse him with
Bel, Booke, and Candle, that so inuisiblie had misused the
Popes holinesse, with the Cardinall of *Pauia*, and the rest of
their company: but *Faustus* notwithstanding made good cheare
with yt which he had beguiled ye pope of, and in the middest
of the order of Saint *Barnards* bare footed Friers, as they were
going on Procession through the market place, called *Campa de
fiore*, he let fall his plate dishes and cup, and withall for a
farwell he made such a thunder-clap and a storme of raine, as

though Heauen and earth should haue met togethei, and so he
left *Rome*....

---

        * monte caual: Monte Cavallo, the Quirinal, upcon
        which Pope Sixtus V had built his palace. P.F.
        confuses the Quirinal and the Capitoline.

How the Emperour Carolus quintus requested of Faustus to see some of
his cunning, whereunto he agreed. Chap. 29.

THe Emperour *Carolus* the fifth of that name was personally
with the rest of his Nobles and gentlemen at the towne of
Inszbruck where he kept his court, vnto the which also Doctor
Faustus resorted, and being there well knowne of diuers
Nobles & gentlemen, he was inuited into the court to meat,
euen in the presence of the Emperour: whom when the
Emperour saw, hee looked earnestly on him, thinking him by
his looks to be some wonderfull fellow, wherfore he asked
one of his Nobles whom he should be: who answered that he
was called Doctor *Faustus*. Whereupon the Emperour held his
peace [page 50] vntill he had taken his repast, after which hee
called vnto him *Faustus*, into the priuie chamber, whither
being come, he sayd vnto him: *Faustus*, I haue heard much of
thee, that thou art excellent in the black Arte, and none like
thee in mine Empire, for men say that thou hast a familiar
Spirit with thee & that thou canst do what thou list: it is
therefore (saith the Emperour) my request of thee that thou
let me see a proofe of thine experience, and I vowe vnto thee
by the honour of mine Emperiall Crowne, none euill shall
happen vnto thee for so dooing. Herevpon Doctor *Faustus*
answered his Maiestie, that vpon those conditions he was
ready in any thing that he could, to doe his highnes
commaundement in what seruice he would appoynt him. Wel,
then heare what I say (quoth the Emperour.) Being once
solitarie in my house, I called to mind mine elders and
auncesters, how it was possible for them to attaine vnto so
great a degree of authoritie, yea so high, that wee the
successors of that line are neuer able to come neere. As for
example, the great and mighty monarch of the worlde
Alexander magnus, was such a lanterne & spectacle to all his

184

successors, as the Cronicles makes mention of so great riches, conquering, and subduing so many king-domes, the which I and those that follow me (I feare) shall neuer bee able to attaine vnto: wherefore, *Faustus*, my hearty desire is that thou wouldst vouchsafe to let me see that *Alexander*, and his Paramour, the which was praysed to be so fayre, and I pray thee shew me them in such sort that I may see their personages, shape, gesture & apparel, as they vsed in their life time, and that here before my face; to the ende that I may say I haue my long desire fulfilled, & to prayse thee to be a famous man in thine arte and experience. Doctor *Faustus* answered: My most excellent Lord, I am ready to accomplish your request in all things, so farre foorth as I and my Spirit are able to performe: yet your Maiestie shall know, that their dead bodies are not able substantially to be brought before you, but such Spirits as haue seene *Alexander* and his Paramour aliue, shall appeare vnto you in manner and forme as they both liued in their most florishing time: and herewith I hope to please your imperiall Maiestie. Then *Faustus* went a little aside to speake to his Spirit, but he returned againe presently, saying: now if it please your Maiesty you shall see them, yet vpon this condition that you demaund no question of them, nor speake vnto them, which the Emperour agreed vnto. Wherewith Doctor *Faustus* opened the priuy chamber doore, where presently entred the great and mighty Emperour *Alexander magnus*, in all things to looke vpon as if he had been aliue, in proportion a strong thick set man, of a middle stature, blacke hayre, and that both thick and curled head and beard, red cheekes, and a broade face, with cyes like a *Basiliske*, hee had on a complet harnesse burnished and grauen exceeding rich to looke vpon; and so passing towards the Emperour *Carolus*, he made lowe and reuerent curtcsie: whereat the Emperour *Carolus* would haue stoode vp to receiue and greete him with the like reuerence, but *Faustus* tooke holde of him and would not permit him to doe it. Shortly after *Alexander* made humble reuerence and went out againe, and comming to the doore his Paramour met him, she comming in, she made the Emperour likewise reuerence, she was clothed in blew Veluet, wrought and embrodered with pearle and golde, she was also excellent fayre like Milke & blood mixed, tall and slender, with a face round as an Apple) and thus shee passed certaine times vp and downe the house, which the Emperour marking, sayd to himselfe: now haue I seene two persons, which my heart hath long wished for to beholde, and sure it cannot otherwise be, sayd he to himselfe, but that the Spirits haue changed themselues into these formes, and haue not deceiued me, calling to his minde the woman that raysed the Prophet *Samuel*: and for that the Emperour would be the more satisfied in the matter, he thought, I haue heard say, that behinde her necke she had a great wart or wenne, wherefore he tooke *Faustus* by the hand without any words, and went to see if it were also to be seen on her or not, but she perceiuing that he came to her, bowed downe her neck, where he saw a great wart, and hereupon shee vanished, leauing the Emperour and the rest well contented.

How Doctor Faustus in the sight of the Emperour coniured a payre of Harts hornes vpon a Knights head that slept out of a cazement. Chap. 30.

WHen Doctor *Faustus* had accomplished the Emperours desire in all things as he was requested, he went foorth into a gallerie, and leaning ouer a rayle to looke into the priuie garden, he saw many of the Emperours Courtiers walking and talking together, and casting his eyes now this way, now that way, he espyed a Knight leaning out at a window of the great hall; who was fast asleepe (for in those dayes it was hote) but the person shall bee namelesse that slept, for that he was a Knight, although it was done to a little disgrace of the Gentleman: it pleased Doctor *Faustus*, through the helpe of his Spirit *Mephostophiles*, to firme vpon his head as hee slept, an huge payre of Harts hornes, and as the Knight awaked thinking to pul in his head, hee hit his homes against the glasse that the panes therof flew about his eares. Think here how this good Gentleman was vexed, for he could neither get backward nor forward: which when the Emperour heard al the courtiers laugh, and came forth to see what was hapened, the Emperour also whe he beheld the Knight with so fayre a head, laughed heartily thereat, and was therewithall well pleased: at last *Faustus*, made him quite of his hornes agayne, but the Knight perceiued how they came, &c.

----

     * firme: fasten

How Doctor Faustus deceiued an Horse-courser. Chap. 34.

IN like manner hee serued an Horse-courser at a faire called
Pheiffring, for Doctor *Faustus* through his cunning had gotten
an excellent fayre Horse, wherevpon hee rid to the Fayre,
where hee had many Chap-men that offered him money:
lastly, he sold him for 40. Dollers, willing him that bought
him, that in any wise he should not ride him ouer any water,
but the Horsecourser marueiled with himself that *Faustus* bad
him ride him ouer no water, (but quoth he) I will prooue, and
forthwith hee rid him into the riuer, presently the horse
vanished from vnder him, and he sate on a bundell of strawe,
in so much that the man was almost drowned. The horse-
courser knewe well where hee lay that had solde him his
horse, wherefore he went angerly to his Inne, where hee
found Doctor *Faustus* fast a sleepe, and snorting on a bed, but
the horsecourser could no longer forbeare him, tooke him by
the leg and began to pull him off the bed, but he pulled him
so, that he pulled his leg from his body, in so much that the
Horse-courser fel down backwardes in the place, then began
Doctor *Faustus* to crie with an open throate, he hath mur
dered me. Hereat the Horse-courser was afraide, and gaue the
flight, thinking none other with himselfe, but that hee had
pulled his leg from his bodie; by this meanes Doctor *Faustus*
kept his money.

*How Doctor Faustus played a merrie iest with the Duke of Anholt in
his Court. Chap. 39.*

DOctor *Faustus* on a time came to the Duke of *Anholt*, the
which welcomed him very courteously, this was in the moneth
of Ianuary, where sitting at the table, he perceiued the
Dutchesse to be with childe, and forbearing himselfe vntill the
meate was taken from the table, and that they brought in the
banquetting dishes, said Doctor *Faustus* to the Dutchesse,
Gracious Ladie, I haue alway heard, that the great bellied
women doe alwaies long for some dainties, I beseech
therefore your Grace hide not your mind from me, but tell me
what you desire to eate, she answered him, Doctor *Faustus*

now truely I will not hide from you what my heart dooth most desire, namely, that if it were now Haruest, I would eate my bellie full of ripe Grapes, and other daintie fruite. Doctor *Faustus* answered herevpon, Gracious Lady, this is a small thing for mee to doe, for I can doo more than this, wherefore he tooke a plate, and made open one of the casements of the windowe, holding it forth, where incontinent hee had his dish full of all maner of fruites, as red and white Grapes, Peares, and Apples, the which came from out of strange Countries, all these he presented the Dutchesse, saying: Madame, I pray you vouchsafe to taste of this daintie fruite, the which came from a farre Countrey, for there the Sommer is not yet ended. The Dutchesse thanked *Faustus* highly, and she fell to her fruite with full appetite. The Duke of *Anholt* notwithstanding could not with-holde to aske *Faustus* with what reason there were such young fruite to be had at that time of the yeare? Doctor *Faustus* tolde him, may it please your Grace to vnderstand, that the yere is deuided into two circles ouer the whole world, that when with vs it is Winter, in the contrary circle it is notwithstanding Sommer, for in *India* and *Saba* there falleth or setteth the Sunne, so that it is so warme, that they haue twise a yeare fruite: and gracious Lorde, I haue a swift Spirit, the which can in the twinckling of an eye fulfill my desire in any thing, wherefore I sent him into those Countries, who hath brought this fruite as you see: whereat the Duke was in great admiration.

----

* Saba: Sheba

How Doctor Faustus shewed the fayre Helena vnto the Students vpon the Sunday following. Chap. 45.

THe Sunday following came these students home to Doctor *Faustus* his owne house, and brought their meate and drinke with them: these men were right welcome guests vnto *Faustus*, wherfore they all fell to drinking of wine smoothly: and being merry, they began some of them to talke of the beauty of women, and euery one gaue foorth his verdit what he had seene and what hee had heard. So one among the rest said, I neuer was so desirous of any thing in this world, as to haue a sight (if it were possible) of fayre *Helena* of *Greece*, for whom the worthy towne of *Troje* was destroyed and razed downe to the ground, therefore sayth hee, that in all mens iudgement shee was more than commonly fayre, because that when she was stolne away from her husband, there was for her recouery so great blood-shed.

Doctor *Faustus* answered: For that you are all my friends and are so desirous to see that famous pearle of *Greece*, fayre *Helena*, the wife of King *Menelaus*, and daughter of *Tindalus* and *Læda*, sister to *Castor* and *Pollux*, who was the fayrest Lady in all *Greece*: I will therefore bring her into your presence personally, and in the same forme of attyre as she vsed to goe when she was in her chiefest flowres and pleasauntest prime of youth. The like haue I done for the Emperour *Carolus quintus*, at his desire I shewed him *Alexander* the great, and his Paramour: but (sayd Doctor *Faustus*) I charge you all that vpon your perils you speake not a word, nor rise vp from the Table so long as she is in your presence. And so he went out of the Hall, returning presently agayne, after whome immediatly followed the fayre and beautiful *Helena*, whose beauty was such that the students were all amazed to see her, esteeming her rather to bee a heauenly than an earthly creature. This Lady appeared before the in a most sumptuous gowne of purple Veluet, richly imbrodered, her hayre hanged downe loose as fayre as the beaten Gold, & of such length that it reached downe to her hammes, with amorous cole-black eyes, a sweete and pleasant round face, her lips red as a Cherry, her cheekes of rose all colour, her mouth small, her neck as white as the Swanne, tall and slender of personage, and in summe, there was not one imperfect part in her: shee looked round about her with a rouling Haukes eye, a smiling & wanton countenance, which neere hand inflamed the hearts of the students, but that they perswaded themselues she was a Spirit, wherefore such phantasies passed away lightly with them: and thus fayre *Helena* & Doctor *Faustus* went out agayne one with another. But the Students at Doctor *Faustus* his entring againe into the hall, requested of him to let them see her againe the next day, for that they would bring with them a painter and so take her counterfeit: which hee denied, affirming that hee could not alwayes rayse vp her Spirit, but onely at certaine times: yet (sayd he) I will giue you her counterfeit, which shall bee alwayes as good to you as if your selues should see the drawing thereof, which they receiued according to his promise, but soone lost it againe. The students departed from *Faustus* home euery one to his house, but they were not able to sleepe the whole night for thinking on the beauty of fayre *Helena*. Wherefore a man may see that the Diuel blindeth and enflameth the heart with lust oftentimes, that men fall in bue with Harlots, nay euen with Furies, which afterward cannot lightly be remoued.

How an old man the neighbour of Faustus, sought to perswade him to amend his euill life, and to fall vnto repentance. Chap. 48.

A Good Christian an honest and vertuous olde man, a louer of the holy scriptures, who was neighbour vnto Doctor *Faustus*: whe he perceiued that many students had their recourse in and out vnto Doctor *Faustus*, he suspected his euill life, wherefore like a friend he inuited Doctor *Faustus* to supper vnto his house, vnto the which hee agreed; and hauing ended their banquet, the olde man began with these words. My louing friend and neighbour Doctor *Faustus*, I haue to desire of you a friendly and Christian request, beseeching you that you wil vouchsafe not to be angry with me, but friendly resolue mee in my doubt, and take my poore inuiting in good part. To whome Doctor *Faustus* answered: My louing neighbour, I pray you say your minde. The began the old Patron to say: My good neighbour, you know in the beginning how that you haue defied God, & all the hoast heauen, & giuen your soule to the Diuel, wherewith you haue incurred Gods high displeasure, and are become from a Christian farre worse than a heathen person: oh consider what you haue done, it is not onely the pleasure of the body, but the safety of the soule that you must haue respect vnto: of which if you be carelesse, then are you cast away, and shall remaine in the anger of almighty God. But yet is it time enough Doctor *Faustus*, if you repent and call vnto the Lord for mercy, as wee haue example in the *Acts* of the Apostles, the eight Chap. of *Simon* in *Samaria*, who was led out of the way, affirming that he was *Simon homo sanctus*. This man was notwithstanding in the end conuerted, after that he had heard the Sermon of *Philip*, for he was baptized, and sawe his sinnes, and repented. Likewise I beseech you good brother Doctor *Faustus*, let my rude Sermon be vnto you a conuersion; and forget the filthy life that you haue led, repent, aske mercy, & liue: for Christ saith, Come vnto me all ye that are weary & heauy loden, & J wil refresh you. And in *Ezechiel*: I desire not the death of a

190

sinner, but rather that hee conuert and liue. Let my words good brother *Faustus*, pearce into your adamant heart, and desire God for his Sonne Christ his sake, to forgiue you. Wherefore haue you so long liued in your Diuelish practises, knowing that in the olde and newe Testament you are forbidden, and that men should not suffer any such to hue, neither haue any conuersation with them, for it is an abomination vnto the Lord; and that such persons haue no part in the Kingdome of God. All this while Doctor *Faustus* heard him very attentiuely, and replyed. Father, your perswasions like me wonderous well, and I thanke you with all my heart for your good will and counsell, promising you so farre as I may to follow your discipline: whereupon he tooke his leaue. And being come home, he layd him very pensiue on his bed, bethinking himselfe of the wordes of the good olde man, and in a maner began to repent that he had giuen his Soule to the Diuell, intending to denie all that hee had promised vnto *Lucifer*. Continuing in these cogitations, sodainly his Spirit appeared vnto him clapping him vpon the head, and wrung it as though he would haue pulled the head from the shoulders, saying vnto him. Thou knowest *Faustus*, that thou hast giuen thy selfe body and soule vnto my Lord *Lucifer*, and hast vowed thy selfe an enemy vnto God and vnto all men; and now thou beginnest to harken to an olde doting foole which perswadeth thee as it were vnto God, when indeed it is too late, for that thou art the diuels, and hee hath good power presently to fetch thee: wherefore he hath sent me vnto thee, to tell thee, that seeing thou hast sorrowed for that thou hast done, begin againe and write another writing with thine owne blood, if not, then will I teare thee all to peeces. Hereat Doctor *Faustus* was sore afrayde, and sayd: My *Mephostophiles*, I will write agayne what thou wilt: wherefore hee sate him downe, and with his owne blood hee wrote as followeth: which writing was afterward sent to a deare friend of the sayd Doctor *Faustus* being his kinsman.

An Oration of Faustus to the Students. Chap. 63.

MY trusty and welbeloued friends, the cause why I haue inuited you into this place is this: Forasmuch as you haue knowne me this many yeares, in what maner of life I haue liued, practising al maner of coniurations and wicked

191

exercises, the which I haue obtayned through the helpe of the diuel, into whose diuelish fellowship they haue brought me, the which vse the like Arte and practise, vrged by the detestable prouocation of my flesh, my stiffe necked and rebellious will, with my filthy infernall thoughts, the which were euer before me, pricking mee forward so earnestly, that I must perforce haue the consent of the diuell to ayde me in my deuises. And to the end I might the better bring my purpose to passe, to haue the Diuels ayd and furtherance, which I neuer haue wanted in mine actions, I haue promised vnto him at the ende and accomplishing of 24. yeares, both body and soule, to doe therewith at his pleasure: and this day, this dismall day those 24. yeares are fully expired, for night beginning my houre-glasse is at an end, the direfull finishing whereof I carefully expect: for out of all doubt this night hee will fetch mee, to whome I haue giuen my selfe in recompence of his seruice, both body and soule, and twice confirmed writings with my proper blood. Now haue I called you my welbeloued Lords, friends, brethren, and fellowes, before that fatall houre to take my friendly farewell, to the end that my departing may not hereafter be hidden from you, beseeching you herewith courteous, and louing Lords and brethren, not to take in euil part any thing done by mee, but with friendly commendations to salute all my friends and companions wheresoeuer: desiring both you and them, if euer I haue trespassed against your minds in any thing, that you would all heartily forgiue me: and as for those lewd practises the which this full 24. yeares I haue followed, you shall hereafter finde them in writing: and I beseech you let this my lamentable ende to the residue of your liues bee a sufficient warning, that you haue God alwayes before your eies, praying vnto him that he would euer defend you from the temptation of the diuell, and all his false deceipts, not falling altogether from God, as I wretched and vngodly damned creature haue done, hauing denied and defied Baptisme, the Sacraments of Christs body, God himselfe, all heauenly powers, and earthly men, yea, I haue denied such a God, that desireth not to haue one lost. Neither let the [page 80] euill fellowship of wicked companions misselead you as it hath done me: visit earnestly and oft the Church, warre and striue continually agaynst the Diuell with a good and stedfast beliefe on God, and Iesus Christ, and vse your vocation in holiness. Lastly, to knitte vp my troubled Oration, this is my friendly request, that you would to rest, & let nothing trouble you: also if you chance to heare any noise, or rumbling about the house, be not therwith afrayd, for there shal no euil happen vnto you: also I pray you arise not out of your beds. But aboue all things I intreate you, if you hereafter finde my dead carkasse, conuay it vnto the earth, for I dye both a good and bad Christian; a good Christian, for that I am heartely sorry, and in my heart alwayes praye for mercy, that my soule may be deliuered: a bad Christian, for that I know the Diuell will haue my bodie, and that would I willingly giue him so that he would leaue my soule in quiet: wherefore I pray you that you would depart to bed, and so I wish you a quiet night, which vnto me notwithstanding will be horrible and fearefull.

This Oration or declaration was made by Doctor *Faustus*, & that with a hearty and resolute minde, to the ende hee might not discomfort them: but the Students wondered greatly thereat, that he was so blinded, for knauery, coniuration, and such like foolish things, to giue his body and soule vnto the diuell: for they loued him entirely, and neuer suspected any such thing before he had opened his mind to them: wherefore one of the sayd vnto him; ah, friend *Faustus*, what haue you done to conccale this matter so long from vs, we would by the help of good Diuines, and the grace of God, haue brought you out of this net, and haue torne you out of the bondage and chaynes of Sathan, whereas nowe we feare it is too late, to the vtter ruine of your body and soule? Doctor *Faustus* answered, I durst neuer doo it, although I often minded, to settle my selfe vnto godly people, to desire counsell and helpe, as once mine olde neighbour counsailed mee, that I shoulde follow his learning, and leaue all my coniurations, yet when I was minded to amend, and to followe that good mans counsell, then came the Diuell and would haue had me away, as this night he is like to doe, and sayd so soone as I turned againe to God, hee would dispatch mee altogether. Thus, euen thus, (good Gentlemen, and my deare friends) was I inthralled in that Satanicall band, all good desires drowned, all pietie banished, al purpose of amendmet vtterly exiled, by the tyranous threatnings of my deadly enemy. But when the Students heard his words, they gaue him counsaile to doo naught else but call vpon God, desiring [page 81] him for the loue of his sweete Sonne Iesus Christes sake, to haue mercy vpon him, teaching him this forme of prayer. O God bee mercifull vnto me, poore and miserable sinner, and enter not into iudgement with me, for no flesh is able to stand before

thee. Although, O Lord, I must leaue my sinfull body vnto the
Diuell, being by him deluded, yet thou in mercy mayest
preserue my soule.

This they repeated vnto him, yet it could take no holde, but
euen as *Caine* he also said his sinnes were greater than God
was able to forgiue; for all his thought was on his writing, he
meant he had made it too filthy in writing it with his owne
blood. The Students & the other that were there, when they
had prayed for him, they wept, and so went foorth, but *Faustus*
taryed in the hall: and when the Gentlemen were laid in bed,
none of them could sleepe, for that they attended to heare if
they might be priuy of his ende. It happened between twelue
and one a clock at midnight, there blewe a mighty storme of
winde against the house, as though it would haue blowne the
foundation thereof out of his place. Hereupon the Students
began to feare, and got out of their beds, comforting one
another, but they would not stirre out of the chamber: and the
Host of the house ran out of doores, thinking the house
would fall. The Students lay neere vnto that hall wherein
Doctor *Faustus* lay, and they heard a mighty noyse and hissing,
as if the hall had beene full of Snakes and Adders: with that
the hall doore flew open wherein Doctor *Faustus* was, then he
began to crie for helpe, saying: murther, murther, but it came
foorth with halfe a voyce hollowly: shortly after they heard
him no more. But when it was day, the Students that had
taken no rest that night, arose and went into the hall in the
which they left Doctor *Faustus*, where notwithstanding they
found no *Faustus*, but all the hall lay besprinckled with blood,
his braines cleauing to the wall: for the Diuel had beaten him
from one wall against another, in one corner lay his eyes, in
another his teeth, a pitifull and fearefull sight to beholde.
Then began the Students to bewayle and weepe for him, and
sought for his body in many places: lastly they came into the
yarde where they found his bodie lying on the horse dung,
most monstrously torne, and fearefull to beholde, for his head
and all his ioynts were dasht in peeces.

The forenamed Students and Masters that were at his death,
haue obtayned so much, that they buried him in the Village
where he was so grieuously tormented. After the which, they
returned to *Wittenberg*, & comming into the house of *Faustus*,
they found ye seruant of *Faustus* very sad, vnto whom they
opened all the mat[t]er, who tooke it exceeding heauilie. There

found they also this history of Doctor *Faustus* noted, and of him written as is before declared, all saue onely his ende, the which was after by the students thereto annexed: further, what his seruant had noted thereof, was made in another booke. And you haue heard that he held by him in his life the Spirit of fayre *Helena*, the which had by him one sonne, the which he named *Iustus Faustus*, euen the same day of his death they vanished away, both mother and sonne. The house before was so darke, that scarce any body could abide therein. The same night Doctor *Faustus* appeared vnto his seruant liuely, and shewed vnto him many secret things the which hee had done and hidden in his life time. Likewise there were certaine which saw Doctor *Faustus* looke out of the window by night as they passed by the house.

And thus ended the whole history of Doctor *Faustus* his coniuration, and other actes that he did in his life; out of the which example euery Christian may learne, but chiefly the stiffenecked and high minded may thereby learne to feare God, and to be careful of their vocation, and to be at defiance with all diuelish workes, as God hath most precisely forbidden, to the end we should not inuite the diuell as a guest, nor giue him place as that wicked *Faustus* hath done: for here we haue a fearefull example of his writing, promise, and end, that we may remember him: that we goe not astray, but take God alwaies before our eies, to call alone vpon him, and to honour him all the dayes of our life, with heart and heartyprayer and with al our strength and soule to glorifie his holy name, defying the Dcuill and all his works, to the end we may remayne with Christ in all endlesse ioy: Amen, Amen, that wish I vnto euery Christian heart, and Gods name to bee glorified. Amen.

finisa.

John Harris began his writing career at age 60, about the same time that he began his teaching career. He lives in Wabasha, Minnesota. His published works currently include:

- *The Epic of Gilgamesh*—an annotated prose rendition pf the ancient epic, based upon original Akkadian, Sumerian, Babylonian and Hittite texts with appendices
- *Faustbook*—a narrative poem in five acts retelling the legend of Faust with a contemporary meaning
- *The Lives and Opinions of Eminent Philosophers, Vol. I & Vol. II*—a collection of short stories and novellas which are predicated upon the lives of certain ancient Greek philosophers, upon which original text this title is based
- *Mrs. Wilson's Tales*—a compilation of authentic tales of the Kathlamet, an extinct native American tribe of the Pacific Northwest, and retold versions of the same tales, cast in the epoch of Wisconsin pioneers of the 18th and 19th centuries.
- *Conscience in Extremis: An Essay on Morality in History*—a book-length essay in consideration of the moral conflicts of the American Sixties with particular emphasis upon the lives of Norman Morrison and Robert S. McNamara, one a martyr and the other an architect of the Vietnam War. The wider question of the import of this epoch to our present and future times is drawn by its analysis and conclusion
- *fishes* – collected poetry
- *The Lore of Gawain* (a compendium of medieval literature),

John is working on Volume III of *Lives and Opinions, a* retelling of the *Lais of Marie de France,* and an untitled essay on the state of public education. More of his writings and podcasts of his books in audio are available at www.ieros.info.

Made in the USA
Middletown, DE
08 March 2019